I'm 16, I'm a witch, and I *still* have to [illegible]

I thought ha[illegible] at my house would [illegible]een this year—but th[illegible]ided to have some fu[illegible] movie monsters part[illegible] guests! And when Libby Chessler crashed the party, I knew I was in for some *real* trouble. I'm going to have to use all my powers to keep this party from becoming too much like a real-life horror movie!

My name's Sabrina and I'm sixteen. I always knew I was different, but I thought it was just because I lived with my strange aunts, Zelda and Hilda, while my divorced parents bounced around the world. Dad's in the foreign service. The *very* foreign service. He's a witch—and so am I.

I can't run to Mom—but *not* because she's currently on an archaeological dig in Peru. She's a mortal. If I set eyes on her in the next two years, she'll turn into a ball of wax. So for now, I'm stuck with my aunts. They're hanging around to show me everything I need to know about this witch business. They say all I have to do is concentrate and point. And I thought fitting in was tough!

You probably think I have superpowers. Think again! I can't turn back time, and I'm on my own when it comes to love. Of course, there are some pretty neat things I *can* do—but that's where the trouble *always* begins. . . .

Sabrina, the Teenage Witch™ books

#1 Sabrina, the Teenage Witch
#2 Showdown at the Mall
#3 Good Switch, Bad Switch
#4 Halloween Havoc

Available from ARCHWAY Paperbacks

Sabrina The Teenage Witch™

Halloween Havoc

Diana G. Gallagher

AN ARCHWAY PAPERBACK
Published by POCKET BOOKS
New York London Toronto Sydney Tokyo Singapore

AN ARCHWAY PAPERBACK *Original*

An Archway Paperback published by
POCKET BOOKS, a division of Simon & Schuster Inc.
1230 Avenue of the Americas, New York, NY 10020

ISBN: 0-671-01436-6

First Archway Paperback printing October 1997

10 9 8 7 6 5 4 3

Cover photo by Don Cadette

Printed in the U.S.A.

IL 5+

For Katie Robertson,
with affection and gratitude
for being a really *good sport!*

Halloween Havoc

Chapter 1

Sighing despondently, Sabrina sipped her orange juice and watched a gangling freshman boy who was desperately trying to cling to the rungs of a telescoping ladder while attempting to attach orange and black crepe paper streamers to the cafeteria's corner wall.

"You've got to go higher, Charles!" The annoyed girl who was spotting the boy on the floor shouted orders without regard for his lack of coordination or the obvious limitations of his precarious perch.

Definitely a junior version of Libby Chessler, Sabrina thought, eyeing the girl with disapproval. With her short, ultrachic haircut, designer jeans, immaculate high-tops, and expensive crocheted vest, the girl dressed to impress. Her domineering tone and aloof expression were further evidence that she had a very high opinion of herself and thought everyone else should, too. Libby, the self-proclaimed and undisputed potentate of the junior class, was just as bossy, arrogant, and intolerant. That similarity and the younger girl's inconsiderate criticism of the struggling boy aggravated Sabrina's unusually gloomy mood.

"It's this high or nothing, Maureen!" Wobbling slightly, Charles let go of the ladder with the hand that also clutched the ends of the crepe paper. Then his foot slipped.

"Sure stick," Sabrina mumbled with a deft point.

Charles grabbed the side strut as his foot found solid purchase on a ladder rung now equipped with a no-slip spell. However, he lost his hold on the streamers as he tightened his grip on the metal support. Clinging to the ladder and groaning with embarrassed dismay, he watched the orange and black ribbons drift down to the floor.

At their current rate of progress, Sabrina calculated with another heavy sigh, it would be Thanksgiving before they finished decorating the Westbridge High School cafeteria for Halloween. It was strictly a ninth-grade project that would culminate in a freshman-only dance on the thirty-first.

"It's a good thing they've got a whole week or they'll never finish." Jenny Kelly, Sabrina's best friend, pushed her long, wavy hair over her shoulder and shook her head.

"They don't have enough help," Harvey Kinkle

observed as Maureen threw up her hands and Charles cautiously crept down the ladder. "We had twenty kids on our freshman decorating committee."

Sabrina nodded absently, lost in her own dismal reflections. The freshmen's Halloween preparations were simply another reminder of how drastically her life had changed since she had turned sixteen and learned that she was a real witch. Ironically, in the case of the haunting holiday, when mortals adopted weird and whimsical personas for fun—the changes were not for the better.

Before she had joined the ranks of the magically empowered, she had enthusiastically embraced Halloween with all its creepy connotations and spooky trappings. As a child, dressing up in an outlandish costume and pretending to be someone or something else for one thrilling night had satisfied an innocent hunger for daring adventure. Courting imagined danger on a trick-or-treat trek through ordinary neighborhoods transformed into dark and mysterious wonderlands had provided a certain chilling anticipation nothing else had ever quite matched.

Remembering, Sabrina sighed.

In junior high, the quest for sugar-coated treasure had been replaced by the equally exciting and terrifying lure of school dances and community-sponsored parties designed to keep preteen ghosts and ghouls focused on fun, food, games, and each other rather than on more mischievous and annoying activities. Vast numbers of trees had been saved from the T.P. blight spread by young and exuberant midnight marauders because of the supervised events, and Sabrina, along with her old friends, had survived their initiations into the initimidating realm of teenaged society without hopelessly branding themselves as uncool social misfits.

And she had always had a good time, too.

Now, however, Halloween filled her with a distinct and deep-seated dread. The trick-or-treaters would pass her darkened doorway without knocking and she would not have the opportunity to attend any parties. Her status as a witch had doomed her to an annual night of unspeakable horror—the traditional family gathering at Cousin Marigold's.

"Witch alert!" Jenny hissed.

Sabrina almost choked on her OJ until she realized Jenny's remark was not a reference to her. Even so, her already abysmal spirits sank several degrees as Libby and Cee Cee, one of her two faithful sidekicks, approached.

Wearing her green and white cheerleader's uniform and carrying a lunch tray, Libby paused to glance imperiously at the fold-out, orange crinkled jack-o'-lanterns and cardboard cutouts of monsters, black cats, and bats piled on the next table. "How utterly tacky."

Cee Cee wrinkled her nose with disdain and

rolled her eyes as Maureen returned for more thumbtacks. "Totally grade school. When *we* were freshmen, the whole cafeteria looked like a haunted house."

"With sound effects," Libby added.

"This is only part of it." Maureen bristled at the older girls' condescending tones. "Tomorrow we're putting in hay bales, corn sheaves, scarecrows, and real pumpkins."

"Oh, great." Tossing her long dark hair, Libby eyed the younger girl contemptuously. "We'll be spending the next week eating lunch in a *barn!*"

Red-faced and fuming, Maureen glared as Libby and Cee Cee made their way to another table across the room. Then she turned on her curious audience and sputtered with indignation. "What's wrong with barns for Halloween?"

Even though Maureen's obnoxious attitude toward Charles warranted a touch of public ridicule, Sabrina felt a pang of sympathy for the girl because the blow had been delivered by Libby, the East Coast champion of caustic comments. But Harvey spoke up before she could think of an appropriate, placating response.

"Nothing. I like barns," Harvey said honestly. "Especially for Halloween."

Sabrina smiled. Handsome and charming with a soft heart, Harvey was her boyfriend and she adored him. She had even passed Drell's true love test to save him from a wretched fate that still made her shudder. Fortunately, Harvey didn't remember that he had almost been condemned to life as a frog after their first sweet but reckless kiss in the front seat of his car. However, Sabrina realized, Maureen was oblivious to the bond of affection between them.

With a dazzling smile, the pretty freshman girl turned to regard Harvey with big brown eyes that gleamed with sudden interest. "We're going to have sound effects, too. And live music at the dance. Cosmic Crunch is, like, the hottest band in the state."

"Cool!" Harvey grinned and nodded, then shrugged. "Too bad it's just for freshmen."

"Yeah," Jenny agreed. "Nobody else is planning anything that I've heard of."

Ignoring Jenny, Maureen sidled closer to Harvey. "Freshmen and their *dates.* We can bring anyone we want."

Sabrina stiffened. Compassionate and easygoing by nature, Harvey was just trying to soothe the girl's ruffled feelings and didn't seem to realize that Maureen was totally misinterpreting his intentions. However, Maureen's intentions *were* blatantly obvious—to her. Even so, she couldn't interfere without coming across as being possessively jealous or implying that Harvey couldn't handle things himself. Scowling, she fisted her finger and resisted the urge to endow the bold Maureen with an odious case of halitosis guaranteed to clear the cafeteria.

"Where's the rest of your decorating committee?" Jenny asked, picking up on the unsettling signals from Maureen, too. She wasn't restricted by the same considerations that prevented Sabrina, the defending girlfriend, from trying to diffuse a potentially uncomfortable situation.

Focused exclusively on Harvey, Maureen did not acknowledge Jenny's question by word or glance. "If you're not doing anything Halloween—"

"I'm busy."

A warm flush of total contentment blossomed on Sabrina's cheeks as Harvey gently took her hand, momentarily overriding her Halloween depression.

Embarrassed by her error in judgment and the rejection, Maureen shoved the card of thumbtacks into the back pocket of her tight jeans, turned, and snapped at her coworker. "Come on, Charles! And don't look so stricken. *I'll* climb the ladder this time."

"Maybe we should just wait until some of the other kids get here," Charles suggested as he trotted across the cafeteria behind the angry girl.

"Stuff it, Charles!"

Totally annoyed, Sabrina pointed again, reducing the depth of the thumbtack card by two-thirds.

"Ouch!" Squealing, Maureen carefully extracted the offending card with its exposed, pointed tacks from her pocket.

Rolling her eyes, Jenny immediately turned to Harvey. "Busy doing what?"

"Yeah?" Sabrina prompted. Even though she couldn't do anything, Harvey hadn't asked about her plans for Halloween yet. She had already decided it would be better to just tell him she had a family obligation she couldn't cancel. Although she had told him the same thing last year, Harvey hadn't questioned her change in plans when her double showed up at his party with instructions to make sure Libby was not left alone with him. However, after the disaster her duplicate had almost caused, which would have irrevocably damaged her reputation and her romantic prospects with Harvey, she didn't want to risk trying that ploy again.

"Nothing, actually."

"Oh." Jenny's lightly freckled face wrinkled with disappointment. "I thought maybe you were going to have another party."

"No way!" Harvey held his hands up. "The only thing that saved me from hosting the most boring bash of the year last Halloween was Libby streaking. And after the teasing she got because of it, I don't think I can count on her to do it again."

Sabrina blinked, struggling not to grin. While she was trying to survive an evening with her ten-year-old cousin, Amanda the Malicious, at Cousin Marigold's in the Other Realm, Libby had convinced Sabrina's not-too-bright copy to streak so Harvey's floundering party wouldn't be a total flop. However, since she had arrived at Harvey's just before the main event and Libby was still outside holding her duplicate's clothes, everyone had assumed Libby had been the bold runner in the buff.

"Would you believe she's still trying to convince everyone it was Sabrina?" Harvey shook his head.

Sabrina just nodded tolerantly. Aside from the fact that there was no way to logically explain an identical twin that no one knew about, she had been talking to one of Harvey's friends when the streaker ran by. Then talking to Harvey himself a few seconds later. Both boys had confirmed that she couldn't possibly have been the streaker, and Libby had suffered the consequences of her devious and determined attempt to humiliate her again. Sabrina was not about to tip the scales of cosmic justice by trying to correct the false assumption. No one would believe her anyway.

"Too bad." Jenny sighed. "That you're not having a party, I mean."

"How come?" Sabrina asked curiously. Even with the infamous streaking incident, Harvey's party hadn't exactly been a huge success.

Jenny shrugged. "Because no one else is, either."

"Really?" Sabrina brightened, then instantly covered her delight with a more somber expression. For her, no parties meant she wouldn't be missing anything socially significant. "Bummer."

"Totally." Jenny sagged and pushed her empty lunch tray aside.

"Maybe not." Harvey glanced at Sabrina and shrugged. "It won't be a total bummer if we spend it together, right? If you and Jenny want to come over to my house, we can watch videos or something after the trick-or-treaters are done driving us crazy ringing the doorbell."

"I guess that would be better than sitting home alone." Jenny sighed again, betraying an enthusiasm quotient that hovered just above zero.

"I can't." Sabrina's enthusiasm quotient *was* zero. "My aunts have this—out-of-town—family thing planned and I've got to go. There's *no* way I can get out of it."

"Now *that's* a bummer." Crestfallen, Harvey sighed. "I guess I'll just watch horror flicks by myself."

"There's no reason Jenny can't come over and watch them with you," Sabrina pointed out magnanimously. "Besides, maybe someone will decide to have some kind of get-together at the last minute."

"That's always possible, I suppose." Resigned, Jenny propped her chin in her hands and shrugged. "And if not, I'll watch Harvey miss you and he can watch me miss the guy I haven't yet met."

"Okay. That's settled then." With an emphatic nod, Sabrina jumped up as the period bell rang, emptied and stashed her lunch tray, and raced for her next class. The old saying that misery loves company flashed through her mind, followed by a distinct feeling of envy. Harvey and Jenny might be spending Halloween alone and miserable, but they didn't have a clue how lucky they were compared to her.

They didn't have to face Amanda, the tiny terror of the Other Realm who miniaturized and collected in jars all the people she didn't like.

It was not an experience Sabrina wanted to repeat.

☆

Chapter 2

☆

The pall of oppressive Halloween dread bearing down on Sabrina got progressively worse as the afternoon wore on. By the time she trudged into the kitchen of her aunts' Victorian house, her spirits were hopelessly mired in a basement of total despair. Not even the ongoing, good-natured, but slightly argumentative repartee between her aunts, punctuated by the bizarre and amusing observations and opinions of Salem the cat, could break through the gloom that enveloped her. However, the sight of a hundred pumpkins of varying shapes and sizes piled on the counters and scattered around the floor did give her pause.

"Let me guess," Sabrina said with a touch of affectionate sarcasm. "Are you trying to corner the market on pumpkins in Westbridge or plotting to take over the town with an army of killer jack-o'-lanterns?"

"This is not funny, Sabrina." Standing by the table, Aunt Zelda shifted an angry gaze back to Hilda. "I want you to get these disgusting atrocities out of this house."

Tongue tucked in total concentration at the corner of her mouth, Hilda remained focused on the pumpkin sitting on the table before her. Happily humming a dark dirge, she sawed away at the misshapen orange globe covered with greenish brown imperfections and deliberately ignored her sister's outraged demand.

"Now!" Thunder boomed as the normally composed and infinitely patient Zelda stamped her foot.

"And in this corner—" Salem muttered. Lying on the edge of the table, the cat flinched as Hilda slammed the knife down.

Startled, Sabrina looked from one annoyed aunt to the other as though following a tense tennis match between volatile rivals.

"They are *not* disgusting, Zelda." Taking a deep breath to stabilize her own wavering composure, Hilda looked up to regard Zelda evenly. "If you weren't so straitlaced and bogged down by dreary tradition, you'd be able to see them for what they really are!"

"And what's that?" Scowling darkly, Zelda folded her arms across her chest.

"Works of art!" Beaming with pride, Hilda turned her latest creation around for Sabrina to inspect. "I call this one 'Jack-O'-Ripper.'"

Sabrina stared at the grotesque face Aunt Hilda had hacked out of the pumpkin's orange flesh. One slanted eye slit was bigger and higher than the other, producing a comical, cross-eyed expression that the triangular nose and crooked mouth with uneven, jagged teeth could not dispel. If she hadn't been so depressed, she would have laughed. All she could manage was a tight smile and an innocuous comment she hoped wouldn't bruise Aunt Hilda's artistic feelings. "It's, uh—different."

"Spoken like a true diplomat," Salem observed. "If you ask me, I think it stinks."

"Nobody asked you," Hilda snapped.

"I meant that literally." Sniffing the pile of stringy pulp and seeds heaped on the table, the cat exhaled violently. "Totally gross."

"It's an abomination!" With a flashing finger, Zelda sent the mutilated pumpkin sliding across the table and off the edge. It hit the floor with a sickening splat and broke into several pieces.

"It wasn't *that* awful," Sabrina said, grimacing. "The eyes were a bit lopsided, but—"

"Hilda's lack of pumpkin-carving expertise is not the issue, Sabrina." Having vented some of her explosive frustrations with the wanton destruction of Jack-O'-Ripper, Zelda sank into a chair. "It's the principle of the thing."

"What thing?" Puzzled, Sabrina dropped her backpack and stepped over an assortment of pumpkins to join them at the table. The seriousness of this difference of opinion between her aunts was both puzzling and disturbing. They often disagreed, but Sabrina had never seen Aunt Zelda come so close to losing it before.

"You are no fun, Zelda." Pointing the pumpkin innards piled beside Salem into oblivion, Hilda pouted.

"Halloween is not supposed to be fun," Zelda countered stiffly, regaining a modicum of controlled indulgence. "It's a time to remember our ancestors—with honor and respect. I will neither condone nor participate in anything that makes a mockery of our deceased ancestors."

"Okay!" Hilda brightened as she levitated an oblong pumpkin from the stack by the door and deposited it in front of her. "You can stay in your room where your inflexible and morbid sensibilities won't be offended. Personally, I seriously doubt that any of our dearly departed will mind if Sabrina and I remember them *and* have a little fun, too."

"I'll mind," the portrait of Aunt Louisa declared.

"There. See?" Zelda nodded curtly to emphasize the point.

"Exception noted." Pleased with her solution, Hilda stared at the blank surface of the pumpkin with a studious frown, then smiled at Sabrina. "Choose your victim."

"If you carve them now, Aunt Hilda, they'll start to rot before Halloween."

"Really?" Hilda grinned. "That will add a certain pungent charm to the festivities, won't it?"

"Mushy *and* stinky pumpkin stuff. The very thought turns my stomach." Gagging, Salem leaped from the table and fled.

"Now see what you've done!" Zelda's eyes flashed. "You've upset the cat."

"He'll get over it."

"What's the point of this argument, anyway?" Sabrina asked glumly. "I mean, what difference does it make whether or not Aunt Hilda carves jack-o'-lanterns when we're all going to be suffering through another Halloween dinner at Cousin Marigold's?"

Both aunts exchanged startled glances.

"Didn't we tell you?" Zelda asked.

"Tell me what?"

"We're not going to Cousin Marigold's." With an exaggerated sigh of disappointment, Hilda shook her head. "And I was so looking forward to doing the gloating this year."

That's certainly understandable, Sabrina thought, hardly daring to believe her ears. She had not been the only victim of abrasive verbal abuse at the family dinner last year. Smug and secure in her marriage to Harold, Cousin Marigold had taken great pleasure in repeatedly reminding her aunts that they were spinsters with little hope of finding husbands or owning Mediterranean villas, and had given no credence to *their* repeated reminders that the absence of both in their lives was by choice. However, Hilda and Zelda had gotten the last laugh. In a moment of intoxicated indiscretion after indulging in too much catnip, Marigold's cat, M'Lady, had let the cat out of the bag.

"She canceled because her divorce from Harold was just finalized," Zelda added.

"You're not kidding, are you?" Sabrina asked.

"I wouldn't dream of joking about Cousin Marigold's humiliation." Zelda smothered a smile behind her hand.

"She lost the custody battle," Hilda explained with feigned solemnity.

"Harold got custody of Amanda?" Sabrina blinked. She really didn't care who the pint-size tyrant lived with as long as she never had to cross paths with the despicable little witch again.

"Quite the contrary. The Witches' Council ruled that Marigold had to keep her!" Picking up the knife, Hilda jammed it into the side of the pumpkin. "As much as I despise Drell, I have to admit he has a sound sense of justice. Marigold has absolutely no hope of finding another husband with that brat around."

"And we won't have to listen to any more snide comments about being single," Zelda added.

Sabrina had stopped listening. Jumping out of her seat, she grabbed her backpack and raced up the stairs. Bursting through the door, she threw her backpack onto the turret-window chair and whooped with excited relief.

"Who pumped you full of joy juice?" Lounging on the bed, Salem eyed Sabrina suspiciously, then yowled as she swept him into her arms, flicked on her CD player, and spun in delirious circles.

"No Cousin Marigold! No Amanda! I'm free—"

Salem groaned as Sabrina suddenly stopped twirling around the cluttered room and dropped him back on the pillows. "Is everyone in this house determined to make me throw up?"

"Sorry." Falling on the bed beside him, Sabrina stared at the ceiling. She was free of the dreaded family obligation on Halloween and no one was having a party! Not that she'd mind watching horror movies with Harvey and Jenny, but it seemed totally unfair not to have something a little more exciting to do after what she had gone through last year.

"Do you experience these drastic mood swings often?" Salem asked cautiously.

Sabrina sighed. "I guess I should be happy just because I won't have to spend Halloween in a jar wondering when the air will run out."

"I would be." Salem gave his black fur a couple of quick licks, then cocked his head. "So what's the problem?"

Turning onto her stomach, Sabrina rested her chin on her folded arms. "No problem. Helping Harvey hand out candy to trick-or-treaters will be fun."

"So is swimming through a swamp—if you're a

snake." Salem shuddered. "Mortals make such a big deal out of Halloween, I can't believe that's your only option."

"It is unless somebody decides to throw a party between now and then. Right now, that doesn't seem likely—" Sabrina rolled over and sat bolt upright. "Unless I do!"

"You? A party here?" Salem's green eyes widened in alarm. "Don't even think about it!"

"Why not?" Sabrina eyed Salem darkly. Since no one else was planning anything special for Halloween, the opportunity to make a successful debut as a hostess on the Westbridge teenage social scene was too good to pass up. She didn't appreciate having her inspired idea rejected by a cat whose definition of a good time was tangling with a ball of yarn and gorging himself with tuna.

Salem glanced toward the door as Hilda and Zelda came down the hall.

"We are not putting fake tombstones on the front lawn, Hilda!"

"They don't have to be fake," Hilda argued. "I can use real ones."

Zelda continued to rant without breaking stride as both women passed Sabrina's open door. "Or stringing spiderwebs on the porch or hanging bedsheet ghosts from the trees. I don't care what everyone else in the neighborhood does."

"Come on, Zelda! Lighten up. Just once I want to celebrate Halloween the way mortals do. Think of it as an educational experience."

"I don't want to talk about it."

"But other witches have fun on Halloween!" Hilda pleaded. "Why can't I?"

"Because."

A moment later, two doors slammed.

"That's why." Salem sighed.

Sabrina frowned thoughtfully. There was no doubt that Aunt Hilda would jump at the chance to have a party.

All she had to do was convince Aunt Zelda.

Selling rowboats on the moon would probably be easier.

Chapter 3

"Is everything okay?" A worried frown creased Harvey's face as he pulled into the driveway of Sabrina's house the next afternoon.

"Uh-huh," Sabrina said absently, staring out the window and pulling her sweater closed against the October chill. The gray overcast skies and low keening of a brisk autumn wind reflected her own troubled thoughts.

Getting through school without mentioning that she was thinking about having a Halloween party had been almost as difficult as trying to figure out the best way to broach the subject with Aunt Zelda. On the drive home, she had lapsed into pensive silence, still stumped about how to proceed. Asking wasn't the problem. Getting yes for an answer definitely was. Even armed with the information she had found in the library, her chances of swaying Aunt Zelda were slim—bordering on hopeless. So she hadn't said anything about the possibility to anyone, not even Harvey. Her social status at Westbridge High wasn't elevated enough to withstand building up everyone's hopes for a dynamite holiday bash and then not being able to deliver. And there was no question that Libby would make sure she never lived down such a disgraceful faux pas.

"You're not mad at me, are you?"

"Me? Mad at you?" Sabrina started, snapping her head around to meet Harvey's warm but bewildered brown eyes. The lock of sandy brown hair that fell over his forehead gave him a slightly rakish look that made her heart flutter. It still amazed her that someone who was so athletically fit and gorgeous could be so honestly nice and caring. She was appalled that he had interpreted her somber mood as anger. "No, I'm just a little preoccupied—with school and stuff."

"Oh. Good. I mean, it's good that you're not mad at me." Nodding, Harvey nervously flexed his hands on the steering wheel. "You've been acting kind of weird the past couple of days."

"I have?"

"Yeah." Relaxing, Harvey draped his arm over the back of the seat. "You've been too quiet. Like you're depressed or something."

"I was," Sabrina admitted. "But I'm over it now. Having dinner with my relatives would have been so boring—" *Not to mention annoying, humiliating, and life-threatening.* "—and I really didn't want to spend Halloween with anyone but you."

"That's how I feel, too." Harvey's winsome smile faltered. "You're sure you won't be bored playing butler to a bunch of neighborhood ghosts and goblins?"

"No! I love trick-or-treaters."

"So do I. To be honest—" Harvey leaned toward her and lowered his voice. "I kind of miss going trick-or-treating myself."

"Yeah. Me too," Sabrina said breathlessly, inhaling softly as Harvey eased closer. She shivered, anticipating the tender kiss, then gasped as the front door slammed and the moment was brutally shattered.

Blushing, Harvey sat back as though he'd been punched.

Irritated, Sabrina looked out the car window and tensed with apprehension.

Aunt Hilda marched down the front steps with a jack-o'-lantern tucked under her arm and her mouth set in petulant determination. Aunt Zelda followed, slamming the door a second time. A gust of wind whipped dry leaves around the yard and across the porch and walk, enhancing the fury brewing between the two women.

"Hilda! Don't you dare put that thing out there!"

Defiantly raising her chin, Hilda turned and

set the plump pumpkin on the bottom step. The ferocious expression had been carved with an exquisite precision and artistry that made Sabrina suspect Hilda had traded in her knife for a spell.

Scampering down the steps, Zelda glared at Hilda, then pointed at the scowling jack-o'-lantern.

Sabrina didn't know if her aunt intended to make the pumpkin disappear, set it on fire, or blow it up. Either way, she wouldn't be able to explain it to Harvey.

"Hey!" Shouting, Sabrina threw open the car door.

Aunt Zelda yanked back her hand, then ran her fingers through her windblown hair.

"Oh, look. It's Sabrina." Hilda shot Zelda a triumphant smile. "And *Harvey.*"

"So I see." Composing herself, Zelda smiled tightly and followed as Hilda hurried over to the car.

Heart racing from the close call, Sabrina stepped out of the car, shut the door, and waved. "Bye, Harvey!"

Hilda opened the door again and peered inside. "Hi, Harvey."

"Uh, hi." Harvey anxiously cleared his throat. "Nice pumpkin."

Crossing her fingers, Sabrina hoped that her aunts' argument wouldn't override their better judgment. They made Harvey edgy. He thought the anxiety was simply a normal reaction to being scrutinized by her somewhat odd but concerned guardians. So far nothing had ever happened to make him suspect just *how* odd they really were. But the odds were that eventually one of them would slip up, and there was only so much strain a teenaged relationship could take, even one that had been authenticated as true love.

"Thank you," Hilda gushed. "I've been practicing."

"She cheats," Zelda said, scowling narrowly.

"Oh." Nodding self-consciously while both women stared at him, one grinning and one obviously not pleased, Harvey valiantly tried to ease the tension he mistakenly thought he had caused. "Well, it looks great, anyway. In fact, your whole house is perfect for Halloween."

"It does have a certain gothic charm, doesn't it?" Hilda glanced pointedly at Zelda. "It would be such a shame not to take advantage of it for the holidays."

"Exactly what I was thinking!" Seizing the opening Harvey and Hilda had inadvertently created, Sabrina blurted out her request. "I'd really love to have a Halloween party. There's nothing else going on this year."

Zelda paled.

"What a nifty idea!" Hilda exclaimed.

"Totally cool!" Harvey grinned.

"Totally," Hilda agreed.

"I don't think so," Zelda interjected.

"But—" Sabrina choked back her protest as her aunts locked stubborn stares.

"Bye, Harvey!" Slamming the car door closed again, Hilda took Zelda by the arm and started back to the house. "Come on. It's family conference time."

Opening the car door again, Sabrina winced apologetically. "Sorry about that, Harvey. I know my aunts act a little strange sometimes, but they're harmless."

Usually.

"No problem. It's just that I can't tell if they like me or not." Harvey shrugged helplessly.

"I'm sure they like you," Sabrina assured him. "Call me later?"

"Absolutely." Shifting into reverse, Harvey reached for the door handle. "And good luck talking your aunts into letting you have that party. This old house of yours would be a ragin' place to spend Halloween."

Maybe too ragin', Sabrina thought as Harvey blew her a kiss and backed out of the drive. As she hurried to catch up with her aunts, she started to wonder if having a party was such a good idea after all. She had been so focused on the chance to achieve social prominence with her peers, she hadn't stopped to consider all the possible ramifications. Her aunts would at least *try* to control their magically eccentric selves in the company of her mortal friends, but the house itself was also a source of the peculiar and unexpected, and it wasn't capable of considering the cataclysmic consequences its actions might cause the young occupant of the upstairs turret room.

As Sabrina rushed through the front door, Zelda pulled free of Hilda's grip and headed for the stairs.

"Where are you going?" Hilda demanded.

"To unwind in a hot tub before I do something I'll regret," Zelda snapped. She raised her finger in warning.

"No. You're coming into the kitchen to discuss Sabrina's problem rationally and with an open mind." Cocking her own finger, Hilda regarded Zelda sternly.

"There's nothing to discuss."

Inserting herself between them, Sabrina attempted to diffuse the explosive situation. "Having a party was an impulsive suggestion. Maybe we should just forget it."

"Nonsense." Convincing Zelda to cooperate with a threatening point at an antique vase she despised and Zelda cherished, Hilda continued through the living room with a grumbling sister and an anxious niece tagging behind.

"I'm only doing this for Sabrina's sake." Kicking a pumpkin out of the way, Zelda took a seat at the kitchen table.

"Who won the jack-o'-lantern war?" Uncurling on the counter, Salem stretched and yawned. "Not that I care."

"We've declared a temporary truce," Hilda announced. "Right, Zelda?"

"For the moment."

"Thank you." Pointing the pumpkin on her chair back into one of Hilda's piles, Sabrina sat down. Being caught in the cross fire between her aunts was unnerving and exhausting.

"Excellent." Sitting down, Hilda waved her magic finger, zapping up a plate of apple-cinnamon doughnuts and three steaming mugs of hot chocolate topped with whipped cream. "Just a little something to take the chill off."

"Off what?" Zelda asked suspiciously.

"The day, the mood—and you, Zelda. You're being very unfair to Sabrina."

"I am not." Stricken, Zelda turned to gaze at her niece. "Am I?"

"Well, maybe. Sort of," Sabrina hedged.

She respected Zelda's feelings and didn't want to offend her, but she couldn't ignore her own needs, either. Even under the best of circumstances, maintaining an illusion of acceptable cool was difficult for any teenager. Trying to counter Libby's constant and derisive campaign to tarnish a tenuous self-image that ranged from freakish to basically okay made the task almost impossible for her. She needed to do something ultracool if she ever hoped to rise above the forces of established and popular power working against her. A Halloween blast that everyone enjoyed would do wonders toward that end. And now that the question of having a party had been put to Zelda and she seemed willing to listen, all Sabrina's earlier misgivings evaporated.

"How am I being unfair?" Zelda pressed with genuine concern.

Hilda answered, "You're forgetting that Sabrina's a teenaged girl trying to cope with a ruthless, judgmental, and unmerciful high school social establishment."

"Tyranny reigns supreme." Salem sighed and stared wistfully into space. "Pardon me while I indulge in a moment of quiet remorse for my lost chance at world domination."

"Aunt Hilda's got it exactly right," Sabrina said, ignoring the once-too-ambitious-warlock-turned cat. "Libby Chessler despises me."

"Having a party won't change that," Zelda said.

"I know. But if everyone else has a great time, it might discredit her."

"She's got a point there, Zelda."

Nodding, Zelda sipped her hot chocolate and deliberated with a vague expression that gave no hint as to which way she was leaning.

Sabrina's desire for the party seemed to intensify in direct proportion to the passing seconds. Riddled with anxiety, she leaned forward expectantly when her aunt finally set her cup down.

"Okay. You can have a party—"

"Yes!" Sabrina was halfway out of her chair before Aunt Zelda finished, bursting her bubble of excitement.

"—but not on Halloween."

"Why not!" Hilda's eyes flashed with indignation. "And don't say because it's disrespectful. Most of *our* ancestors were notorious for having more than a little fun at mortal expense on Halloween."

"That doesn't make it right," Zelda countered stubbornly. "It's a travesty how the meaning of Halloween has gotten so distorted over the centuries."

"Wrong!" Sabrina jumped in with her historical ammunition in a last desperate attempt to change Zelda's mind. "Originally Halloween was an ancient Celtic holiday called the *Festival of Samhain.* And a festival, according to the dictionary, is a celebration."

"Merrymaking!" Grinning, Hilda raised her mug of hot chocolate in a salute.

"Party!" Salem looked up sharply. "I don't suppose I could talk you into serving tuna pâté?"

Noting how Aunt Zelda suddenly sat up and took notice, Sabrina continued with an energized fervor reminiscent of the ancient Irish enthusiasm for the holiday. "Costumes and jack-o'-lanterns and trick-or-treat can *all* be traced back to those beginnings."

"Someone's been doing their homework," Hilda observed with approval.

"Yeah, I did." On a roll, Sabrina pressed. "The Celts believed that the way between this world and the other world was thrown open on Halloween so that spirits could wander among mortals. They wore masks and disguises to trick the ghosts into believing they were ghosts, too."

"With good reason." Hilda rolled her eyes. "Ghosts are worse than witches when it comes to playing pranks on mortals on Halloween."

"Quite true," Zelda agreed.

"Which is why no one wanted them hanging around in the mortal realm indefinitely," Hilda said.

"Right!" Sabrina beamed. "They put lanterns in their windows to make sure the spirits could find their way *back* to the other world."

"Jack-o'-lanterns," Hilda said, just in case Zelda had missed the point. "Mine stays."

"It seems to me," Sabrina concluded, "that *not* having a party would be going against tradition."

"Another excellent point, Sabrina." Hilda reached for a doughnut. "So if Zelda won't let *you* have a party, maybe I'll invite a few of my friends over. *Witch* friends."

"You wouldn't!" Zelda gasped.

"Don't bet on it." Taking a bite, Hilda chewed with calculated nonchalance.

"Are you threatening me?" Zelda fumed.

"Yep." Swallowing, Hilda grew serious again. "But I'll pass in favor of Sabrina."

"Please, Aunt Zelda."

"Is it really that important to you?" Zelda asked, her demeanor softening.

Sabrina shrugged. "Yeah, it is. Especially since

there's nothing else going on except a freshman dance that no upperclassman would be caught dead attending—"

Hilda choked on her hot chocolate. Salem groaned and Zelda stiffened.

"Sorry." Sabrina plunged ahead despite her insensitive slip of the tongue. "What I mean is—everybody *expects* to have a great time on Halloween. If I have a party, it's practically guaranteed to be a smash success."

Sighing, Zelda nodded. "All right."

Sabrina started to rise out of her chair again but stopped herself when Zelda raised a cautionary finger.

"But—no one breathes a word of this to anyone from the Other Realm." Zelda's gaze targeted Hilda. "Not one word."

"My lips are sealed," Hilda promised gravely. "I hate moving."

"Moving?" Sabrina blinked. "What's that got to do with anything?"

"Living with neighbors who think we're a little weird is one thing." Draining her cup, Hilda grimaced. "Living with neighbors who are convinced the house is haunted and that we're responsible for every little disaster that comes along—natural or supernatural—is impossible. We had to leave Hampton Beach in a hurry in 1893 after Aunt Vesta literally raised the roofs of every house on the street."

Sabrina stared at them aghast. "She didn't."

"She did." Zelda sighed wearily. "And turned all the picket fences upside down. When it comes to Halloween mischief, witches have a tendency to get a bit carried away."

"Creating glorious chaos wherever they go." A fleeting look of longing dawned on Hilda's face. "Aunt Louisa used to put scarecrows in the stocks and make the pumpkin crop stampede down Main Street back in colonial Salem."

The portrait snickered.

Hilda sighed. "A lot of witches don't share Zelda's stodgy and boring ideas about the proper way to observe Halloween."

"And who can blame them?" Chuckling, Salem leaped from the counter to the table. "Mortals set themselves up to be scared senseless on Halloween."

"The truth is, normal people love it when something inexplicable and bizarre happens," Hilda said. "The scarier and weirder, the better."

"Maybe, but Sabrina's party is off-limits." Zelda looked from Hilda to Salem, then back to Hilda again. "Agreed?"

Stunned by the casual confessions of random and rowdy misconduct by the witch community on Halloween, Sabrina just stared at them in speechless horror.

"All right." Salem's tail twitched in agitation. "I'll keep my mouth shut and I won't try to engage any of Sabrina's friends in idle conversation. No one listens to cats, anyway."

"Mum's the word." Hilda raised her right hand, then noticed Sabrina's stricken expression. "Don't worry, Sabrina. Your party will be the talk of the town for months to come. Years, maybe!"

"That's what I'm worried about," Sabrina muttered, but no one was listening.

"As long as we're going to do this, we might as well do it right." Now that she was committed, Zelda launched into planning for the holiday bash with earnest zeal. The yellow pages appeared in front of her with a flick of her finger. "Who do we know that could recommend a decent caterer?"

"How about someone who specializes in pizza with anchovies and caviar?" Salem purred.

Hilda was already off on her own tangent, sorting pumpkins by size and shape, and didn't respond.

All Sabrina could think about was the night Jenny had come to sleep over. If not for some quick thinking and a rare decree of compassionate concession from Drell, Jenny would have been doomed to stay a grasshopper after she stumbled into the Other Realm through the linen closet.

Sabrina shuddered with a different dread. Harboring any hope that she could invite thirty-plus teenagers to the house for a party and not have *something* go wrong was sheer folly.

☆

Chapter 4

☆

To Sabrina's intense relief, the entire weekend had passed with nothing stranger happening than Harvey catching Aunt Hilda lighting her jack-o'-lantern Friday night. At the time, the incident had seemed like an ill omen, warning of even more ruinous calamity to come. Now, as she sat in American History first period Monday morning, thinking back on it, she had to smile.

Watching through the window in the door, Sabrina saw Harvey pull into the driveway and opened the door as he raced up the walk toward the porch. They had decided to catch the latest action thriller at the multiplex and he was running a few minutes late.

"Oops! I almost forgot." Snapping her wrist as she walked through the front foyer, Aunt Hilda ordered the candle in the pumpkin she had put on the steps that afternoon to burst into flame. "Light my fire!"

Sabrina gasped.

With a startled yelp, Harvey jumped back from the porch to avoid being singed by the gigantic tongues of flame that roared through the pumpkin's facial holes. The pulpy underside of the cutout top sizzled as it baked to a charred crisp in a single spectacular second. "Drastic!"

Hidden behind the door, Hilda shrugged apologetically. "Guess I'd better turn it down a little, huh?"

"If you don't mind," Sabrina hissed.

Watching Hilda's pumpkin flambeau in open-mouthed awe, Harvey grinned as the fingers of fire suddenly coalesced into a small, sputtering candle flame. The blackened, shriveled top fell inside with an anticlimactic *plop.*

"Hi, Harvey."

"Hey, Sabrina!" With a backward glance at the jack-o'-lantern, Harvey bounded up the steps. "How'd you do that?"

"Uh—"

"Remote control." Hilda stepped into view, holding a small black device in one hand and a compact fire extinguisher in the other. "I've been dabbling in pyrotechnics, but I haven't quite got the hang of it yet. Sorry."

"Don't be," Harvey said. "That was totally impressive."

"Please. Don't encourage her." Slinging her bag over her shoulder, Sabrina took Harvey's arm and rushed him back down the steps before Aunt Hilda decided to try some other special effect she couldn't explain so easily. "Come on, or we'll miss the beginning of the movie."

"So what did your aunts decide about the party?" Harvey asked as he opened the car door for her.

Sabrina hesitated. She was still trying to decide if seizing the chance to make a prestigious social impact was worth the very real risk of making an impact that would irrevocably and definitely *prove* she was the weirdo freak Libby so diligently claimed, rather than keeping everyone guessing. Her aunts meant well and they would honestly try to curtail their supernatural impulses. Even so, they were witches, and using magic was second nature. Aunt Hilda's flaming pumpkin trick was a perfect example of what she could expect. Remaining in undistinguished social obscurity seemed preferable to setting herself up for a fall into social oblivion.

"It's still under discussion." Sabrina slid into the front seat. "So don't say anything to anyone yet. Okay?"

"Sure." Settling into the driver's seat, Harvey started the engine, then frowned thoughtfully. "You know what would be really cool?"

"What?"

"If everyone came as a character from their favorite horror film." Harvey's face lit up with an enthusiasm that rivaled Aunt Hilda's pumpkin inferno. "We could rent all the old movies and have them running on the TV. Maybe even have a contest for the most accurate costume."

"I'll think about it."

"You should," Harvey said, suddenly serious. "I'm pretty sure my Halloween party almost bombed because except for wearing costumes, there wasn't anything that made it different from any other party during the year."

"I'll definitely think about it."

Actually, Sabrina thought, *having a theme isn't a bad idea.* However, the question of whether to take the plunge still hadn't been decided.

"Whenever you're ready, Ms. Spellman." The history teacher, Mr. Dunkirk, impatiently eyed Sabrina over the rim of his thick glasses.

"Uh—" Faltering as her attention was rudely called back to the present, Sabrina smiled wanly. "Would you repeat the question?"

"The Boston Tea Party was—" Mr. Dunkirk's stare bored into her as he paused, expecting her to complete the ambiguous sentence.

Taken by surprise, Sabrina voiced the first thing that popped into her mind. "By invitation only?"

Mr. Dunkirk started as muffled laughter rippled through the room.

The bell blared.

Saved, Sabrina thought, hoping her embarrassed flush wasn't too noticeable.

"Indian costumes required." Jenny giggled as she picked up her books and fled for the door with Sabrina hard on her heels.

"Speaking of costumes," Harvey said, joining them in the safety of the hall. "Have your aunts made up their minds about your Halloween party?"

"You're having a party?" Jenny exclaimed. Her green eyes widened with delight, then narrowed uncertainly. "Why didn't you tell me?"

"Because—"

"A party?" Libby jumped in front of them from behind, her dark eyes flashing with outraged indignation. Flawlessly coordinated in a short tweed skirt, matching jacket, and honey gold turtleneck, she glared at each of them in turn. "Who's having a party? Where? When? Why wasn't I informed?"

Cee Cee and Jill, Libby's ever-present shadows, appeared out of nowhere to flank their fearless and furious leader.

Sabrina's heart palpitated wildly with the realization that the moment of decision was upon her. Faced with her best friend and her boyfriend, both of whom would rather go to a Halloween bash than pass out candy and watch movies, and the most powerful girl in school, who loathed her but whose sanction would guarantee that everyone who was anyone would attend, there was no way out.

No other parties were being planned.

If she didn't come through, Halloween in Westbridge would be a total bust for the junior class.

And now Libby knew. The cheerleader would not hesitate to let everyone else know that Sabrina could have rescued them from a dismal Halloween with nowhere to go and nothing to do—and didn't. The stigma would be indelibly etched on her reputation.

"My aunts finally gave in this morning. Eight o'clock at my house Halloween night."

The point of no return. Sabrina sighed through a tight smile. Her fate—whatever it turned out to be—was sealed.

"Yes!" Jenny squealed, then calmed herself when she caught Libby's contemptuous glance.

"Too cool." Harvey grinned. "Wait until you see Sabrina's aunt's fire-breathing jack-o'-lantern!"

"Then I take it we're invited, too?" Libby asked, raising a perfectly plucked eyebrow.

"Of course." Sabrina smiled tighter. "The theme is monster movies."

Harvey beamed. "Yeah! Come as any character you want. Monster or heroine."

Mad scientist, Sabrina thought, noting Libby's cold and guarded expression. She was always hatching some kind of diabolical plot to advance her own interests. However, despite their mutual dislike and the added pressure of having Libby's outspoken and critical presence on the premises, not inviting her would be a disastrous error in judgment. The cheerleader set the pace and almost everyone else followed. Sabrina hoped she'd lead them right to the Spellmans' front door Friday night.

"It's an intriguing concept," Libby conceded without committing herself.

"You're not actually thinking about going?" Cee Cee asked with unconcealed astonishment.

Jill paled.

"I'll certainly give it serious consideration." As she moved down the corridor, Libby looked back with a sly smile. "Later, Sabrina."

"Later." Sabrina shifted uncomfortably.

"Do you think they'll come?" Jenny asked, looking slightly stunned because Libby hadn't flatly refused the invitation.

"They'll be there," Harvey said with absolute certainty. "Sabrina's party is the only game in town. No way Libby's gonna miss it."

"You're probably right." Jenny sighed and cast a sympathetic glance at Sabrina. "You do know that she'll spend the whole night finding fault with every little thing, don't you?"

Sabrina nodded. In an ideal world, Libby would come down with the flu at the last minute. Almost as unlikely but just as good, she might actually enjoy herself and neglect to point out that in her opinion, the music was just as stale as the chips. Realistically, however, Sabrina's best bet for offsetting the effects of Libby's complaints was to make sure that everyone else was having too much fun to hear or care.

"Too cool!" Libby grinned as she led her entourage around the corner out of Sabrina's sight and hearing.

"Cool?" Cee Cee repeated sarcastically. "A party at Sabrina's?"

"Why on earth would you even think about going, Libby?" Jill huffed with irritation. "If you go, we'll have to go, too!"

"Unfortunate, but true." Cee Cee's dark curls bounced as she shivered with disgust. "That old house of hers gives me the creeps. Besides, I just hate the idea of giving Sabrina our stamp of approval by showing up."

"Don't worry," Libby snapped, annoyed by Cee Cee and Jill's lack of creative cunning. "I have no intention of going."

"Oh, well, that's a relief." Cee Cee's bright smile slowly faded into a puzzled frown. "So what are we supposed to do instead? Sit home alone?"

Libby looked at the stylish dark-haired girl as though she had suddenly gone insane, and sneered. "Not hardly."

"But nobody else is planning anything," Jill whined. "Everyone will be at Sabrina's."

"Believe me, Jill—" Pausing outside the door of their next class, Libby smiled with conniving confidence. *"No one* will be at Sabrina's on Halloween."

Heading down the hall toward her locker, Sabrina intercepted Lauren Wentworth and Casey Hill leaving their last class. Although they weren't on the same trend-setting level as the cheerleading squad, both girls were members of the student council, and were active in track and volleyball and well liked in general. More important, they had always been pleasant and friendly to her, even when Libby had tried to make her early days at Westbridge High totally miserable. It was the first time she'd seen them all day and she quickly extended invitations.

"A Halloween party, huh?" Casey nodded, her bland expression betraying an interest level slightly less than mildly curious.

"On Friday night? Well, I, uh—" Lauren faltered, as though she didn't quite know what to say.

"The theme is monster movies," Sabrina added nervously, distressed by the girl's hesitation. Lauren and Casey weren't the only kids who had reacted to the news of her party with a measure of enthusiasm that fell somewhere between lukewarm and frigid. Driven by a growing sense of uneasiness, she tossed out a few additional incentives. "My aunts are going all out. We'll have all the latest CDs and gift certificates for the best costumes, and it's being catered by Orlando's."

"Orlando's, huh?" Casey continued to nod.

Lauren grimaced with repulsion. "We have to come dressed like monsters?"

"No, not necessarily," Sabrina assured her. "There's all kinds of cool-looking female villains—"

"Sorry, Sabrina, but we've really *got* to get going." Grabbing Lauren by the arm, Casey pulled her toward the exit. "Thanks, though. For the invite!"

Brushed off or what? Sabrina continued on to her own locker, pondering the disturbing lack of excitement she seemed to be getting from everyone about her party. Was it possible Libby's attempts to keep her bottomed out on the socially acceptable scale had been more effective than she realized? As unlikely as it seemed, she couldn't dismiss the notion that a large majority of the kids she had invited would rather do nothing than attend a bash at her house.

"Hey, Sabrina!" Ned Wallace, editor of the school paper and starter on the basketball team, waved as he hurried past. "How's it going?"

"Great!" Sabrina quickened her pace to catch up to him. "I've decided to have a Halloween party Friday night—"

"Yeah?" Ned's angular face brightened. "What time?"

"My house. Eight o'clock."

"Thanks for letting me know. The prospects for Halloween this year were looking pretty bleak." Smiling broadly, Ned broke into a jog. "Later!"

Then again, maybe she was being overly sensitive and paranoid. Just because everyone didn't display Jenny's unrestrained and exuberant eagerness didn't necessarily mean they weren't interested. Perhaps they were just too concerned about their exterior cool to show it.

Stashing the books she didn't need in her locker, Sabrina looked up as Jenny came dashing around the corner and skidded to a breathless halt.

"Sorry I'm late, Sabrina. I wanted to catch Brad Shaefer while I had the chance."

Pulling back slightly, Sabrina gazed at her flushed and excited friend with open surprise. "Just about every girl in school wants a chance to catch Brad Shaefer. Except me, of course."

"That's *not* what I meant. Sweaty, glory-seeking jocks are not my type. I just wanted to tell him about your Halloween party."

Sabrina jerked back again. "And did you?" Having the captain and star quarterback on the Westbridge High varsity football team agree to grace her party with his esteemed presence would carry almost as much weight as Libby's endorsement. The rest of the team took their cues from Brad, blindly and without question.

"Yeah!" Jenny nodded vigorously.

"How'd you manage that?" Pulling out her jacket and slamming the locker closed, Sabrina started toward the exit. She had a lot to do before Friday night and only four nights and four days left to do it.

Exhilarated by her audacity, Jenny explained in a rush. "It wasn't that hard, actually. I just hung around outside the boys' locker room until he showed up for practice. And then I just told him."

Sabrina eyed her askance.

"Don't worry. I didn't beg or anything. I just kind of casually mentioned that you were having a party and he and his friends were welcome to come."

"So what did he say? Is he coming?"

"He said he'd *definitely* keep it in mind." Thrilled, Jenny pushed through the outer doors and laughed aloud as a brisk breeze blew her long hair back from her face.

"So he didn't actually *say* he was coming."

Jenny shrugged. "No, but he didn't say he *wasn't* coming, either."

"That's something, I guess. Thanks, Jenny."

"No problem!" Grinning, Jenny fell into step beside her. "I have the strangest feeling that this party of yours is going to be a total blast."

"I hope you're right." Casting a wary eye on the dark clouds gathering in the eastern sky, Sabrina sighed. Although Jenny's spirits weren't dampened by the cold and gloomy October afternoon, she couldn't shake her own mounting feelings of foreboding or stop worrying. No matter how hard she tried to carry on as normally as possible in the midst of the absurd, disaster dogged her every effort with the tenacity of a bloodhound, aided and abetted by her various wonderful but weird relatives.

Despite their promises and best intentions, her aunts could spoil everything with a thoughtless flick of an index finger. A practical joker by nature, Salem wouldn't be able to keep his mouth shut all night or refrain from playing a prank or two on her unsuspecting guests. Confined in her portrait, Aunt Louisa was limited in the amount of damage she could do, but that wouldn't stop her from trying.

However, none of that would be a problem if nobody showed up.

Chapter 5

Wandering down the main concourse of the mall Thursday afternoon, Sabrina listened as Jenny fretted about her costume for Friday night. Pressed to get all the last-minute details taken care of for the party, she had her own problems and was growing impatient with Jenny's stubborn focus on her futile search.

"This is so frustrating!" After fuming for a moment, Jenny glanced at Sabrina with apologetic chagrin. "Sorry. You've been so frantic getting ready for tomorrow night, you probably haven't had time to get your costume together, either."

"Actually, I'm all set, but how come you put yours off until the last minute?"

"I didn't. I've been collecting stuff all week. I just never thought putting together a gypsy costume would be so hard!" Jamming her hands into her jacket pockets, Jenny sighed in defeat. "I've got most of it, but every time I go into a store asking for a peasant blouse, the sales clerk looks at me like I just beamed in from another planet."

"Peasant blouses haven't been in style for years."

"I know that!" Jenny huffed. "I came to the mall as a last resort. I've already tried every thrift store within twenty-five miles."

Sabrina didn't understand why Jenny had her heart set on coming to the party dressed as the gypsy girl from the old black-and-white movie *The Wolfman,* but she was, and they were running out of precious time.

"What about that secondhand nostalgia store that's on the same block as the Slicery?" Hiding the sudden smile that followed a sudden flash of brilliant inspiration, Sabrina latched on to a plan that would solve Jenny's problem and expedite her own errands.

"The Penny Loafer?" Jenny nodded. "I checked it out Tuesday. Actually, I found a couple of scarves, a bunch of bracelets, and a long, dark skirt there."

"Well, since I've got to stop by the Slicery to get gift certificates for the costume contest anyway, maybe we should check it out again."

"What's the point? I was just there two days ago."

Point *being the operative word,* Sabrina thought with impish glee.

"Not that I expect to win one of those gift

certificates," Jenny said wistfully, "but it would be nice to look as authentic as possible. Who's judging the contest, anyway?"

"My aunts said they would, but they promised to make themselves scarce the rest of the time." Sabrina didn't add that the family cat would have the tie-breaking vote. Or that since she had created exact replicas of Morticia and Gomez Addams's movie wardrobes for herself and Harvey with a mere wave of her magic hand, they were excluding themselves from the contest in the interest of fairness. (And that movie was more of a comedy anyway.) Harvey, however, thought he was opting out because he had agreed to be her cohost. "Harvey and I won't be competing, though."

"A wise decision," Jenny agreed. "Then no one can accuse your aunts of being partial."

"Exactly." And since a blouse didn't constitute Jenny's entire outfit, Sabrina didn't have to worry about giving her best friend an unfair advantage, either. And although helping people with magic didn't always work out as she expected, she didn't see how conjuring a peasant blouse could possibly backfire and cause any harm.

More harm might be done if she didn't get home to supervise her aunts, who had volunteered to decorate the house. Even though they had agreed to do things the mortal way using the decorations she had bought, anything could happen. Now that Aunt Hilda's preoccupation with jack-o'-lanterns had run its course and the front walk and porch looked like the staging area for a pumpkin parade, there was no telling what other outrageous ideas would strike her fancy. She had stopped pestering Zelda about erecting tombstones on the lawn, but that didn't mean she had given up. Even worse, in deference to the deceased, Aunt Zelda was pushing for a more somber setting that would totally expunge anyone's festive inclinations the moment they walked in the door.

"Your aunts wouldn't happen to have an old peasant blouse tucked away in a closet, would they?"

"I don't think so, but maybe the Penny Loafer got a big shipment of new old stuff in over the past couple of days."

"Including a pcasant blouse?" Jenny grinned despite her distress. "You're a hopeless dreamer, Sabrina."

"Maybe, but I promise you'll have one for tomorrow night. Even if I have to make it myself. So relax, okay?"

"I didn't know you could sew!"

"Magic fingers!" Eyes sparkling, Sabrina raised her hand and wiggled her fingers. As she expected, Jenny laughed at the implied joke and her smile was a welcome relief. Suffering from preparty anxiety all week, Sabrina was having enough trouble keeping her own mood buoyant and cheerful without having Jenny's depression dragging her down, too. Even though Aunt Zelda had assured her that everyone planning a big social event needlessly worried themselves to distraction, she just couldn't dispel the feeling that something terrible was going to happen.

"Isn't that Libby?"

Like Libby.

Pausing, Sabrina peered through the glass door of Hennigan's Costume Emporium. The shop was mobbed with people in for final fittings or picking up costumes they had reserved in advance. Standing at the counter, Libby put her change away, then casually removed her teeth.

"A vampire," Jenny quipped with a sardonic grin. "How appropriate."

Sabrina stifled a startled laugh with her hand as the cheerleader held up the gleaming plastic teeth with pointed canines to admire them. Dropping them in a bag the harried clerk shoved toward her, Libby turned to leave.

"Come on, Jenny. Show's over and I've still got things to do, including trying to find your blouse." Too stressed to trade insults with Libby and hold her own at the moment, Sabrina tugged on Jenny's sleeve.

"No, wait a minute. Maybe they've got one in here." Executing a sharp turn to the right, Jenny barged into the costume shop.

"Can't hurt to ask, I guess," Sabrina muttered as she followed.

Like every store in the mall, Hennigan's was decorated to the hilt for Halloween. Moving skeletons and lighted jack-o'-lanterns rested on black shrouds draped in windows framed by strings of blinking pumpkin lights. Bats and small ghosts that made eerie sounds when the door opened dangled from the ceiling, and plastic black widow spiders crawled across gossamer webs stretched in corners. The excessive commercial splendor was rivaled only by the glittering gaiety of the Christmas season that would deck the mall's halls beginning November first.

"Well, imagine meeting you two here." Blocking the aisle, Libby eyed Sabrina and Jenny with curious delight. "The selection of cool costumes is getting pretty slim, though. I'm afraid you may have to settle for something totally mundane and tasteless."

"If the fangs fit—" Jenny smiled.

"Bite me!" Libby snapped, her temper flaring.

"We're just browsing," Sabrina said before the exchange escalated and words were fired that couldn't be ignored. "So if you'll excuse us, Libby, we're kind of in a hurry."

"Of course." Regaining her calm as quickly as she had lost it, Libby nodded with understanding and actually smiled. "You must be running yourself ragged getting everything ready for the big bash tomorrow night."

Wondering what ulterior motive Libby could

possibly have for being so suspiciously civil, Sabrina lied. "No. Everything's pretty much under control."

"Sabrina's aunts hired a caterer," Jenny added.

"So I've heard. Orlando's, right? He has an impeccable reputation. Expensive, too." This time, Libby's smile was infused with a distinct and disquieting trace of smug pleasure. "Catch you later." Still smiling, Libby sauntered out of the store as though she had just pulled off a major coup.

"She's up to something, Sabrina." Jenny frowned. "Any idea what?"

"Not a clue." As Jenny headed to the counter to ask about the blouse, Sabrina sighed. Whatever nasty scheme was brewing in Libby's devious mind, she'd find out about it soon enough. On the up side, word about the caterer had apparently been spreading through the grapevine, which meant that her party was a subject of discussion, which also meant that people were more interested than they were letting on. Maybe Libby had just decided to go with the flow and not buck the tides of popular opinion that preferred to go to a party—any party—rather than stay home on Halloween.

Maybe.

If there was a way to sabotage her social debut and get away with it without damaging herself, Libby would.

"No luck, Sabrina." Jenny returned looking more despondent than before. "They don't even have a gypsy costume I can rent."

"Let's get a move on, then. You still have to get a tambourine at Exclusively Acoustics, and the Penny Loafer closes at five-thirty."

As they headed toward the door, Jenny graciously tried to let Sabrina off the hook. "You don't have to go with me, Sabrina. You've got too much to do."

"Don't worry about it." Sabrina appreciated Jenny's concern, but dismissed it with a casual wave. Without her, Jenny wouldn't find the peasant blouse because it wouldn't be in the Penny Loafer until she pointed it into existence. Unlike the orderly chain stores in the mall that carried only the latest styles, the nostalgia store was stocked so full of old clothes of all kinds, no one would question the sudden appearance of a blouse that was exactly what Jenny wanted, at a fabulously low price, and that she had obviously overlooked on Tuesday.

And except for the Slicery gift certificates, there wasn't anything left undone Sabrina couldn't finish with magic if she had to.

All the little final preparations were the least of her troubles, Sabrina realized as she spied Tracey Lopez and Casey Hill in the mall. They were headed straight for the costume shop—until they saw her and Jenny on their way out.

Moving in tandem as though manipulated by an invisible puppeteer, both girls suddenly swerved and walked on by without looking back.

There was no doubt that they had deliberately wanted to avoid running into her.

The big question was, why?

Chapter 6

With the peasant blouse safely in Jenny's deliriously grateful possession, and the Slicery gift certificates purchased, Sabrina arrived home just after six. The scene that greeted her shoved all her worries about Libby's unknown intentions concerning the party to a remote corner of inconsequence in her mind. She couldn't have been more staggered if her aunts had changed the front door into a stone portal guarded by a snarling gargoyle, converted the foyer into a cave complete with bats and water-dripping stalactites, and placed a giant cauldron filled with the bubbling, smoking chartreuse concoction they fondly referred to as Hocus-pocus Punch in the middle of the living-room floor.

Gasping as she stepped into the foyer, Sabrina looked around in dumbfounded despair. All the decorations and supplies she had spent so much time finding and choosing were scattered, strewn, piled, draped, strung, tacked, and taped in haphazard disarray from one end of the house to the other. Creased and stretched orange and black crepe paper streamers, which should have been gently twisted and looped from corners to central spots on the ceiling, drooped and dangled from random points without regard to symmetry. A four-foot hinged cardboard skeleton was tacked to the coat closet door with its skull, arms, and legs skewed at awkward angles. A selection of hard plastic monster masks, intended as instant costumes for anyone who might need one, were taped over a string of orange lights on the front window so the bulbs shone through the eyeholes.

Too mind-boggled to survey the chaotic confusion in any more detail, Sabrina asked numbly, "What is going on?"

"We're decorating the house for your party." Aunt Zelda looked up from the foldout cardboard and crepe paper black cat she was trying to clip together. An assortment of lopsided, smashed, and ripped honeycomb pumpkins she had already mutilated littered the carpet around her. "Like mortals, just as we promised."

Sitting on the stairs, Salem pulled a piece of cellophane tape off his tail with his teeth. "Welcome to holiday crafts for the creatively challenged. If you value your sanity, stay out of their way."

Creatively incompetent is more accurate, Sabrina thought as she stepped over a half-finished haunted house with a torn roof and the porch piece tabbed together wrong side out. Hilda and Zelda's pathetic decorating efforts made Maureen and Charles look like pros.

Wearing tangled loops of crepe paper, Aunt Hilda waved from the top of the baby grand piano. The section of torn and tortured streamers she had just taped to the ceiling fell at her feet, ignored as she frowned at her stricken niece. "You look kind of pale. You're not coming down with something, are you?"

"Have you been running around with your coat unbuttoned?" Aunt Zelda chided gently as she picked at the honeycombed crepe paper she had crushed with the plastic clip. "October is the worst month for catching cold."

"That's the truth." Tearing a piece of cellophane tape off a holder, Hilda rolled it into a circle and picked up the fallen streamers. "Sunshine and blue skies and bone-chilling winds. A very unhealthy combination if you're not careful."

"I'm, uh, just—tired." Holding back tears of fatigue, frustration, and nerves, Sabrina smiled wanly. Her aunts were only trying to help. Getting upset would hurt their feelings and wouldn't undo the damage that had already been done. "I see you've been busy."

"Hmmm." Brow wrinkled in concentration, Zelda attempted to attach the black cat to a standing cardboard full moon. The connecting tab ripped and the cat's crepe paper body crumpled in her fumbling hands. Sighing, she tossed the whole mess over her shoulder and grabbed another cat that was still safely inside its plastic package.

"I hope that isn't a trend." Muttering, Salem sniffed one of the ruined foldout pumpkins and gave it a tentative bat with his paw. As the paper pumpkin bounced across the carpet, he bounded after it. *"Bonzai!"*

"Why don't you let me do that?" Sabrina reached for the package in Aunt Zelda's hand. Although salvaging one black cat wouldn't make any difference whatsoever given the scope of the decoration destruction her aunts had been pursuing with such enthusiastic and inept abandon, Sabrina had to do something to prevent herself from having a complete nervous breakdown on the spot.

"Not necessary, Sabrina." Smiling as she tore open the plastic wrapping, Zelda held up a staying hand. "I think I'm getting the hang of it now."

"I wish I could say the same." Disengaging from the strands of crepe paper wrapped around her shoulders and legs, Hilda jumped off the piano and eyed the sadly sagging streamers she had finally managed to secure. "Mortals make this decorating business look so easy. How do they do it?"

"Patience and practice, I'm sure." Flipping open the black cat, Zelda took a plastic pin and carefully connected the cardboard ends to keep the rounded crepe paper body in place. "There! Look. I did it without mushing this crinkly stuff."

Still in attack mode, Salem came bounding back and took a flying leap into the pile of torn and squashed honeycomb pumpkins. Claws extended, he swung a lethal paw and snagged the newly assembled cat from Zelda's hand. Sharp feline fangs sank into the crinkly stuff, mushing it beyond redemption.

"Taking up the slack, huh, Salem?" Sinking onto the couch, Sabrina sighed in weary defeat.

"Tough day?" Hilda placed a hand on Sabrina's forehead, then smiled. "No fever. Good thing. A dose of my home-pointed cold remedy does wonders for stuffy noses and coughs, but the side effects leave a lot to be desired."

"What side effects?" Sabrina asked for future reference.

"It causes hives and makes your hair fall out," Zelda explained.

"And nobody loves a bald cat covered with red welts." Losing interest in the mangled foldouts, Salem jumped onto the couch. "Trust me."

"Sounds as bad as spellfluenza," Sabrina said,

remembering how she lost her powers when she caught the flu. "Remind me not to catch a cold."

"That's why my remedy is so effective." Hilda grinned. "Everyone makes sure they don't get sick to begin with."

Rising off the floor, Zelda stretched. "Well, I must say, trying to decorate the mortal way has been extremely entertaining, but I've had it."

"Me, too." Surveying the wrack and ruin of their Halloween handiwork, Hilda heaved a satisfied sigh. "But it was fun."

Feeling sick to her stomach but afraid to say anything for fear Aunt Hilda would ply her with a home-brewed nausea medicine that would blacken her teeth or worse, Sabrina just sat in devastated silence. She could fix everything with a simple point, but her aunts were so proud of themselves, she didn't have the heart. Determined to give her a strictly mortal party with no magical shenanigans or snafus, they had taken the time and trouble to decorate the house the way everyone else did. She just hadn't expected them to fail so miserably.

"Do you want to cook or finish up in here?" Zelda cast a questioning glance at Hilda, who frowned thoughtfully for a second.

"As much as I despise kitchen drudgery, I'll cook. Besides, your artistic skills could use some fine-tuning."

"Deal." Taking a deep breath, Zelda closed her

eyes and raised her arms as she chanted. "Halloween pumpkins, ghosts, and bats, be as you were before; deck the house with bones and cats and finish the party decor!"

Stunned, Sabrina stared as every torn and crushed decoration that had been hung or flung aside was swept into the maelstrom of a frenzied tornado wind that grew in proportion to the amount of debris it consumed. Clamping her hands over her ears to dampen the roar, she watched as the funnel whipped around the living room, a swirling kaleidoscope of orange and black. When it vanished with a whoosh a few seconds later, the living room and entrance hall had been decorated exactly as she envisioned.

"Fantastic!" Laughing, Sabrina gazed at the perfect display with shining eyes.

"I think so." With a cocky nod, Zelda placed her hands on her hips. "What do you think, Hilda?"

"Not bad," Hilda admitted, "but your spell was a bit overdone. A simple point would have accomplished the same thing."

"Perhaps, but I thought the circumstances demanded something more dramatic. If I were Sabrina, I would have thrown an absolute fit over the mess we created. But she didn't say a word."

"Didn't want to hurt our feelings, huh?" Hilda asked with an amused smile.

"No, but—" Delighted but bewildered, Sabrina

shook her head. "Why did you spend all afternoon decorating without magic when you obviously intended to use magic to make everything right in the end?"

"Because we promised to decorate the house like mortals," Hilda said matter-of-factly.

"And we did," Zelda added.

"But we *didn't* promise to stick you with the results." Grinning, Hilda waved her index finger with a flourish. "Dinner's ready and I'm famished after all that cutting and taping. Let's eat."

"I'll be there in a minute," Sabrina said, feeling too drained by anxiety, relief, and exhaustion to move just yet. "And thanks."

"You're welcome." Waving over her shoulder, Hilda disappeared into the dining room.

Aunt Zelda paused halfway to the door. "We just want this party of yours to be a success, Sabrina. No matter what it takes."

"I appreciate everything you've done, Aunt Zelda. Especially since I know how much Halloween means to you."

A playful smile crept onto Aunt Zelda's face. "To be honest, I've always wanted to just let my hair down and have a good time on Halloween, too. I was just too set in my serious ways to admit it."

"Yeah?" Sabrina brightened. "Cool!"

"But don't you *dare* tell Aunt Hilda." Frowning slightly, Zelda pointed a warning finger.

"Not a word."

"Good. If she even *suspects* that I'm not as opposed to having a little fun on Halloween as she thinks I am, there'll be no controlling her. I will not be responsible for unleashing her impetuous imagination on our helpless mortal neighborhood."

As Zelda winked and left to join Hilda for dinner, Sabrina settled back to admire the final phase of her aunts' decorating spree. The crepe paper streamers were twisted, looped, and centered with absolute precision. Blinking orange lights framed the windows, casting a cheerful orange glow on delicate cotton spiderwebs that looked remarkably like real ones. The plastic masks were stacked on the hall table with the finished haunted house. Clusters of honeycombed crepe paper pumpkins, ghosts, bats, and cats accented by sprigs of colorful autumn leaves were arranged here and there, lending a festive flair to the room without being too overbearing.

All in all, Sabrina thought as she started to doze off, the party was shaping up better than she had dreamed possible. Even though no one was talking to her, everyone at Westbridge High was talking to each other about it. Her aunts were cooperating, and Orlando's had confirmed. The house was decorated, and her costume, as well as Harvey's and Jenny's, were hanging in their respective closets. The final details, a diversion she hoped would take the edge off her last-minute jitters, would be taken care of in a flurry of excited anticipation tomorrow evening.

There was nothing left to do now but wait.

And worry.

As Sabrina curled up on the couch beside Salem and slipped into a restless sleep, Libby's enigmatic and sinister smile flashed through her mind.

☆

Chapter 7

☆

Still wearing her school clothes, Sabrina raced out of her room and headed for the front stairs. Halloween had finally arrived and Orlando was due any minute to set up the dining-room table with trays of finger foods and exotic snacks guaranteed to delight all teenaged palates regardless of acquired tastes for less refined fare. It was just after six, but he had sworn that kept on ice, everything would stay fresh for hours. Sabrina hoped so for his sake. Stricken with an acute case of preparty fright and raw nerves, she didn't trust herself to refrain from turning him into a slug if anything went wrong.

So far, since her aunts had magically undone the decoration disaster the previous afternoon, nothing else had gone awry. Oddly enough, that just made her more nervous than if they had been plagued by a string of calamities. Whatever the something was that was bound to go wrong, it was still lurking in the wings waiting to happen.

"How do I look?" Aunt Hilda stood in the entrance foyer, her face glowing with excitement.

Taken by surprise, Sabrina stopped halfway down the stairs and gawked.

Holding a crystal globe in one hand and a slim gold wand in the other, Hilda spread her arms and turned in a circle for inspection. Her dark blue cape with crescent moons, fiery suns, and stars embroidered in glittering gold flared out as she twirled, revealing a floor-length dark blue tunic underneath. A belt made of engraved and linked metal squares fastened by tasseled cords hung loosely around her waist. The costume and her short blond hair were topped off by a pointed hat that matched the cape and bent slightly backward at a fold two-thirds up its height.

"I'm waiting." Hilda's lilting voice rose in expectation.

"You look like Merlin the Magician," Sabrina said flatly.

The light in Hilda's eyes dimmed as her face wrinkled into a disappointed pout. "You don't like it."

"No, I do. It's a great costume." Even though she was totally stressed out, Sabrina rushed down the remaining steps to soothe her aunt's bruised feelings. "It's just that Merlin isn't a monster or a character from a monster movie."

"But he can be!" Brandishing the golden wand with a sweeping wave of her hand, Hilda disappeared with a whuffing sound and a flash of smoking light.

When the smoke cleared a split second later, Sabrina jumped back onto the first step with a startled cry.

A fire lizard measuring twelve feet long from the end of its smoking nose to the tip of its barbed tail filled the foyer. Unfolding greenish gold leathery wings, the creature drew back a narrow triangular head, screeched, then exhaled. Jets of flame spewed from its mouth and its slitted golden eyes glittered.

"Be careful, Hilda!" Aunt Zelda admonished sharply from the living room. "You'll singe the woodwork!"

"Sorry."

Hearing Hilda's voice emanating from the ferocious beast shattered the tension that had been building in Sabrina all day. Laughing, she collapsed on the steps and wiped tears from her eyes. "I don't get it."

The dragon morphed back into a gratified Aunt Hilda. "Merlin was a shape-shifter."

"I don't think that qualifies, but it doesn't matter," Sabrina conceded. Hilda had graciously agreed to take on the trick-or-treat duty, leaving her and Aunt Zelda free to deal with Orlando and any other last-minute fussing that seemed necessary. She could wear whatever she wanted.

"You're right." Hilda nodded emphatically. "It doesn't matter. Except for judging the costume contest, Zelda and I are going to spend most of the night in the kitchen keeping the food and drink flowing. And staying out of your way. I dressed up to astound and delight the neighborhood kids."

"What's your definition of astound?" Sabrina asked warily.

With an uncertain grin, Hilda flicked her wand at the jack-o'-lantern resting on a high stool by the stairs. Specks of light that resembled Fourth of July sparklers crackled and sputtered inside it, then fizzled out. "About like that?"

Sabrina frowned thoughtfully, then blinked in astonishment as Aunt Zelda walked in. For some reason she hadn't expected her more sedate aunt to get into a costume. She certainly hadn't expected to see Zelda wearing a gorgeous white brocade gown with hoopskirts and carrying a silver star–tipped wand in her white gloved hand. A tiara crowned her blond hair, which fell in curling cascades to her shoulders. "Don't tell me. Glinda the Good Witch of the North."

"Right! From *The Wizard of Oz.*" Executing an elegant curtsy, Zelda winked. "L. Frank Baum did so much to enhance our image by including a good witch in his story, I couldn't resist. And it *was* a movie."

Sabrina just smiled. Both her aunts had put a

lot of time and effort into doing everything mortally and magically possible to make her party a success. They could dress as Tweedle-Dum and Tweedle-Dee if they wanted, but she'd settle for Merlin and Glinda.

The front doorbell rang.

"They're here!" Hilda gasped and looked around the foyer in a near panic.

"Who is?" Sabrina's heart leaped into her throat. She wasn't expecting Harvey and Jenny until seven forty-five, an hour and a half from now and fifteen minutes before the party officially started.

Then the back doorbell rang.

"That must be Orlando." Lifting her full skirts off the floor, Zelda turned and hurried toward the kitchen. "He's late."

"Only by seven minutes." As Sabrina jumped up to follow Zelda, Hilda grabbed her by the arm.

"Don't leave, Sabrina. I don't know what to do!"

"About what?"

The doorbell rang again and the muffled sound of a tiny voice seeped through the heavy door. "Trick or treat!"

"About them! Your Aunt Zelda's been dragging me from one family function to another on Halloween for centuries. I've never done this before."

Surrendering to Hilda's panicked plea, Sabrina sighed. Aunt Zelda and Orlando could manage without her for a few minutes while she gave Hilda a crash course in twentieth-century trick-or-treating practices. "There's nothing to it. Where's the bowl of candy?"

"Candy?" Hilda winced. "I forgot."

"Trick or treat!"

"Just a minute!" Desperate, Hilda set the crystal globe on the high chest by the door, then snapped the wand, conjuring a high eight-legged stand shaped like a black widow spider. A huge orange bowl filled with wrapped treats appeared on top of it. "Okay. There's the candy. Now what?"

Picking up the bowl, Sabrina glanced at the silver foil candy wrappers and rolled her eyes. "Magic Munchies?"

Hilda shrugged. "I was in a hurry. They're just chocolate-covered caramel crunch."

Sabrina opened the door just as a man and two small children were heading back down the steps.

"Come on, kids!" the man snapped impatiently. "The fight starts in fifteen minutes and I don't want to miss the opening round. Figures your mom would have to work late tonight."

"Wait a minute!" Sabrina called. "Don't go without your treats."

Hilda cracked the door wider and peeked around the edge.

"Okay!" Spinning around, the boy rushed forward with his hand out. Wearing a one-piece discount-store pirate outfit and carrying an empty plastic grocery bag, he flipped his mask up and peered into the bowl. "Magic Munchies? Yuck. Never heard of 'em."

"They were special ordered," Hilda quipped, moving into view. "Deal with it."

A younger girl dressed as a princess held her mask and empty sack in one hand and clung to her father's leg with the other.

"You shouldn't turn on your porch light until you're ready," the man grumbled as he half dragged and half coaxed the little girl back up the steps.

"Sue me," Hilda muttered under her breath. She smiled tightly when Sabrina nudged her with her elbow.

As Sabrina dropped a candy into the boy's bag, a piercing yowl rang out in the darkness.

Flinging her mask and bag into the air, the little girl grabbed her father's jeans with both hands and screamed in short, painful bursts of high-pitched terror. Her father looked up just as Salem came racing up the walk, dashed between his legs, and hightailed it through the open door. Unbalanced and startled with his daughter's arms wrapped around his leg, the man stumbled and fell.

"Ohmigosh!" Handing Hilda the bowl, Sabrina ran to assist. "Are you all right?"

Furious, the man frowned, unable to hear her over the girl's shrill cries.

Flicking her finger, Sabrina lowered the decibel level to a tolerable range. Surprised, the frightened girl blinked and stopped screaming to sob quietly instead.

"Here. Let me help you up."

"Don't bother!" Shaking her off as Sabrina reached for his arm, the man stood up, then moaned when he tried to put weight on his foot.

"What's the matter?" Hilda stepped out of the doorway onto the porch, clutching the candy bowl in front of her.

"I think I sprained my ankle." Hobbling, the man turned around and sank onto the steps. Prying his daughter's hands off his jeans, he glanced back. "I hope you've got good homeowner's insurance because I *am* going to sue."

"I didn't mean that literally." Scowling, Hilda sent the candy bowl skimming back to the spider stand with an annoyed wave when the man looked away.

The young pirate gasped. "How'd you do that?"

"Magic or wires," Hilda returned casually. "Take your pick."

"Cool!"

"Maybe you just twisted it a little," Sabrina said anxiously. She just wanted the man and his kids to go away so she could turn her full attention to the party. "It'll probably be fine in the morning."

Craning her neck to peer over Sabrina's shoulder, Hilda pointed at the man's ankle, then spoke with forced sweetness. "It's probably better already, so let's just drop all this talk about suing, shall we?"

"Forget it, lady." Standing up again, the man tested his ankle and winced. "Great. Thanks to your cat, I'm crippled and Connie and David are going to miss out on trick-or-treating, too."

"No way!" David shouted. "You promised!"

"I want my candy," Connie wailed.

"I'll be lucky if I can manage to limp home," the man snapped. Taking Connie's hand, he glared at Hilda. "You'll be hearing from my lawyers. Unless—"

"Unless what?" Hilda frowned.

The man shrugged. "I'd be willing to forget this whole thing if your daughter there will take my kids around the neighborhood for an hour or so."

"Not a chance!" Sabrina gasped, then stumbled as Hilda grabbed her arm and pulled her toward the door.

"Don't go away," Hilda said brightly. "We'll be right back."

"I can't go trick-or-treating," Sabrina protested hotly as Hilda closed the door. "The party starts at eight and I'm not even dressed yet! Why can't we just fix his ankle and send them on their way?"

"I did," Hilda hissed back. "But there's nothing to stop him from suing us anyway—except taking those poor little kids on their candy rounds."

"He just wants to get home so he doesn't miss some stupid prizefight on TV." Fuming, Sabrina glanced at Salem as he casually sauntered down the stairs. "Thanks a lot, Salem. What was your problem, anyway?"

"Obviously," Salem said sarcastically, "you've never been pursued by a gang of grade-school thugs intent on bagging a black cat for who knows what ill purpose on Halloween."

"What were you doing outside in the first place?" Hilda asked with no trace of sympathy.

"I do have a life!" Arching his back in indignation, Salem leaped through the railing and disappeared around the corner, muttering to himself. "And if my calculations are correct, I still have about six of them left."

"So!" Forgetting the cat, Hilda turned back to Sabrina. "Will you take them?"

"But I've got things to do!"

"All of which will take you about ten seconds and a few flicks of your finger," Hilda reminded her. "Including getting into your costume. And to be honest—"

"What?" Sabrina asked more sharply than she intended.

"Walking around the neighborhood for an hour

will be infinitely more beneficial than bustling around here getting on everyone's nerves. Believe it or not, Zelda can handle Orlando. And now that I've seen how it's done, I can manage the trick-or-treaters." Hilda hesitated. "I think."

Sighing, Sabrina nodded. In a way, the entire incident was a relief. Something had finally gone wrong. With luck, the powers of fate that enforced Murphy's Law—that what could go wrong would go wrong—would be satisfied with this irritating but relatively minor glitch for the rest of the night.

"What?" Salem huffed. "No shrimp stuffed with crab?"

"Orlando!" Aunt Zelda called frantically over the sound of glass and metal crashing to the floor. "Where are you going?"

"You did not inform me that you had a cat, madam!" Orlando declared with a clipped and pretentious European accent. "I am allergic to cats!"

Grabbing Sabrina's arm again, Hilda dragged her to the door and shoved her outside before she could press another argument. The man and his children waited at the base of the steps. "Deal!"

Sabrina smiled lamely.

"We live right around the corner. One-six-two Hudson Street. See you in an hour." The man waved and limped off down the walk at an impressive pace.

David pulled on the corners of his mouth with

his fingers, stuck out his tongue, and crossed his eyes.

Connie started to cry.

Then again, Sabrina thought forlornly, if Murphy was insatiable, her party was a smorgasbord of opportunity for catastrophe.

☆

Chapter 8

☆

My feet hurt!" Connie grumbled loudly.

"Don't be such a baby!" Pulling his mask down over his face and shining his flashlight on the dark sidewalk, David stomped ahead of Sabrina and his younger sister. "Girls!"

"It's not much farther, Connie." Sabrina sighed, barely masking her annoyance. "Your house is just around the corner."

"We're almost done?" Whining, the spoiled little princess balked and stamped her foot. "But he's got more candy than me!"

"No, he doesn't," Sabrina said, her patience wearing thin as she got Connie moving again. David hadn't stopped teasing Connie, who hadn't stopped complaining, during the entire forty-five minutes they had been tramping from one house to another. "Your bag is bigger, so it just doesn't look as full."

"It's not as full," the girl insisted petulantly.

"Well, it'll have to do. I've got to get home."

"I don't want to go home!" David called back as he reached the corner of Hudson and Park. "Let's go this way!" Looking up and down the street and finding it clear of traffic, the boy bolted across the intersection instead of turning toward his own house.

"David! Get back here!"

"Make me!" David laughed from the opposite corner.

Don't tempt me, Sabrina thought hotly as the boy ran toward the nearest house, a shadow moving through the night with a circle of light marking his forward progress.

Scowling and sniffling, Connie pulled free of Sabrina's hand and stopped in the light cast by an overhead streetlamp. Tucking her flashlight under her arm, she peered into her bag.

"Come *on,* Connie," Sabrina urged sharply as she hurried forward into the dark, hoping the girl would follow. With less than an hour remaining before her party started, she wasn't going to cater to the whims of her uncooperative and ungrateful charges any longer.

Connie sat down, dumped her candy onto the sidewalk, and began counting the pieces. "One, two, three . . ."

Exasperated, Sabrina turned to deal with David. With an emphatic point, she targeted his flashlight beam to stop him in his tracks and set him on a return course. "Freeze, please! Retreat feet!" Then she turned back to Connie.

The girl started a second pile when she got to ten, which was apparently as high as she could count. "One, two—"

"Put your candy back in your bag, Connie. You can count it when you get home."

"—three, four—"

"Hey! What's happening? Help!"

Whirling at the sound of David's hysterical voice, Sabrina threw up her hands. The flashlight beam jumped erratically as the boy's arms flailed in a desperate attempt to stop himself from moving backward down the walk. Pointing again, Sabrina modified the spell. "About-face! March!"

Executing a perfect pivot, David continued moving down the walk facing forward. Since Connie was stubbornly engaged with candy counting and not likely to run off, Sabrina kept a wary eye on the boy to make sure he got back across the street safely. No cars approached as he stepped off the curb and marched toward her in wide-eyed shock, clutching his flashlight and bag of candy to his chest lest the mysterious force manipulating his legs decided to snatch the bag from his greedy grasp.

"Out of the way, kid!"

Alarmed by the impatient demand, Sabrina looked back. A group of older kids dressed in various combinations of torn jeans and T-shirts splattered with something red to resemble blood, and black leather with metal studs and chains, came into the light behind the oblivious little girl sitting cross-legged on the sidewalk. Despite their wild, teased, and colored hair and the camouflage designs painted on their sullen faces, Sabrina guessed they were about twelve or thirteen years old. Not old enough to give up a chance to collect free candy or run amok in the neighborhood, but certainly old enough to make allowances for a four-year-old.

Diligently separating her candy into piles, Connie paid no attention as three girls and one of the boys walked by her in single file, rolling their eyes in vexed disgust. When the second, larger boy paused beside her, she continued to count without acknowledging the intruder.

". . . Seven, eight, nine—"

For a kid her age, Sabrina thought as she started back toward Connie, *her ability to tune out and focus is awesome.*

"Stupid kid!" Drawing his leg back, the boy aimed a kick at Connie's neat little piles. "You don't own the sidewalk—"

Sabrina's finger was infinitely faster than the bully's foot. Hidden in the moonless dark, she invoked a silent spell. The boy yelped in terror when an invisible power grabbed his raised foot as it swung forward, then spun him around.

"Something's got my foot! Help! It's got—" Thrown off balance, the boy pitched forward onto the adjacent lawn.

Unaware of why their friend had fallen, the other preteens laughed uproariously.

"Nice try, Jon, but you can't spook us!"

"Dork!"

Connie looked up with mild interest, then immediately returned to the task at hand as the boy scrambled to his feet. Breathless and shaken, he eyed Connie warily and gave her a wide berth as he dashed around her and raced across the side street.

Hanging back out of the dim light, Sabrina indulged in a moment of justified pleasure. She flatly rejected the unsettling idea that she had succumbed to the witchy impulse to have a little fun with a mortal just because it was Halloween and she could get away with it. The bullying boy, like the disobedient David, had deserved a good scare.

But she had to admit it had been fun, too.

"Sabrina! Help!" David yelled as he stepped out of the street onto the sidewalk behind her. "Something's moving my feet! I can't stop my feet!"

The four older kids gaped at him openmouthed, glanced nervously at each other, then ran after Jon with astonishing bursts of speed.

That problem solved, Sabrina stepped back into the light where David could see her. Placing her hands on her hips, she glanced up and around. "Leave my friend alone, you stupid old ghost!" Shaking a warning finger for effect, she frowned and demanded sternly, "I'm warning you, ghost. Get out of here or I'll—" With a quick flick, she released David's legs.

David came to an abrupt halt with the beam of his flashlight shining on his face. A huge smile suddenly replaced his expression of stunned fright as he took a tentative step and realized he was in control again. "Wow! That was totally weird! Was that really a ghost?"

Sabrina shrugged. "Maybe. It *is* Halloween. And it's getting late. Let's go."

David didn't argue as he moved up beside her. "So how'd you make it go away? I want to know. Just in case it ever happens again."

"Just be firm and don't act scared," Sabrina said seriously. "It's no fun picking on someone who's not afraid. The same thing works with people, too."

"Got it." Giving Sabrina a thumbs-up, David scowled at his sister, who was now counting the piles.

Sighing, Connie looked at Sabrina. "How much is ten piles of ten pieces plus one pile of ten pieces plus eight pieces?"

"One hundred and eighteen. Now pick up your candy so I can get you home."

As Connie scooped up her take and stuffed it back into her bag, David glanced at his bag and frowned. "I wonder how many I've got."

"I'm sure Connie will be happy to count them for you," Sabrina said wearily. "Later. At home."

Taking off down Hudson Street with both kids in tow, Sabrina realized that Aunt Hilda had been right. She did feel more relaxed. After she dropped the kids off, she could discreetly *pop* herself home, change in a matter of seconds, and still have plenty of time to check out all the preparations before Harvey and Jenny arrived.

Even the nagging worry about something going wrong had vanished. A quick point could solve any unexpected problem that arose. Besides, Aunt Hilda was probably having too much fun astounding a steady stream of trick-or-treaters to create any mischief in the house, and her persuasive and capable Aunt Zelda had surely placated the allergic and temperamental Orlando. Although she wasn't thrilled knowing that food by the famous local chef was the main attraction and reason, second only to the absence of anywhere else to go, a lot of kids had decided to come to the party, but at least they were coming.

"How'd you do that, lady?"

"It's a secret." Hilda winked at the small boy dressed as a Starfleet Academy cadet from *Star Trek.* Throwing herself totally into the role of wizard, she had just created a particularly dazzling display of Halloween magic. Distracted by the smoking jack-o'-lantern that had literally blown its top in a shower of crackling, sizzling sparks, the cadet's hand still hovered over the candy bowl. The short Klingon standing behind him stared in silent awe as the pumpkin top dropped back into place.

"Do it again!" Recovering, the cadet fished a Magic Munchie out of the pumpkin bowl and stepped back to wait in eager anticipation.

Watching from the porch railing, Salem yawned.

"Sorry. Only one trick and one treat per customer." Holding the bowl out to the alien warrior, Hilda choked back a chuckle as he fumbled for a candy without taking his eyes off the pumpkin. Unable to resist, she casually pointed at the jack-o'-lantern that had been the main source of thrilling fun for the neighborhood kids all evening. Even the parents had been impressed and no one had seriously questioned how the pumpkin's entertaining antics had been rigged.

Still smoking, the pumpkin spoke in a deep, eerie voice. "Welcome to the Burning Zone."

"Whoa! Cool!" The cadet grinned.

"Boring," Salem said, stretching. "There's a definitive lack of inspired variety in your repertoire of spells, Merlin."

Dropping his treat, the junior Klingon stumbled backward toward the steps. With a lightning-fast flash of her finger, Hilda steadied the startled boy so he didn't fall. One twisted ankle per Halloween was enough.

The cadet stared at Hilda in fascination, assuming she was a ventriloquist as well as a magician. "Gosh. Your lips didn't even twitch!"

"Practice makes perfect." Spotting two teenagers coming up the walk, Hilda started. Although both were dressed in regular clothes, the boy wore gruesome makeup that made his facial skin look as if it was rotting off the bone. The girl's face was white with dark lines and shadows that accented her eyes but did not detract from her pretty features. Certain the young zombies were early arrivals for Sabrina's party, Hilda frantically tried to think of a delaying tactic. Her niece wasn't home yet, and she didn't want to let anyone in until the nervous hostess was there to greet them. However, when the boy paused and shouted at two smaller children who had fallen behind, she realized that no excuse was necessary.

"Hurry up or we're going home now!"

Annoyed, the white-faced girl snapped, "If we're late getting to Libby's party because of your brother and sister, Mark, I'm going to be totally mad. And you'll be totally sorry."

Libby's party?

"Did I hear that right?" Looking alert for the first time in an hour, Salem sat up.

Hilda waved him to be quiet, her attention focused on the zombies, who were too preoccupied with their own problems to notice.

Mark nudged the girl. "Shhh. This is Sabrina's house."

Wincing, the girl nodded. "Oops."

Holding her temper in check, Hilda gave the cadet and his Klingon sidekick another Munchie, then sternly ordered them to leave. "Now. Before I turn you into toads."

The Klingon ran.

Waving, the cadet looked back as he ambled down the steps. "You're totally awesome, lady. Bye."

Setting the pumpkin bowl on the black spider stand by the door, Hilda quickly decided on a course of action as a much younger girl wearing a homemade witch costume and an even smaller boy dressed in a white sheet with a plastic ghost mask dangling around his neck caught up to the teens. She hissed at the cat, "Go get Zelda."

"I'd rather *get* Libby," Salem hissed back as he jumped off the railing.

"Exactly what I had in mind," Hilda muttered as the cat scampered through the door. Waving her hand, she instantly conjured a variety of impressive props, including a coffin, a rickety rocking chair, and a stack of blank tombstones. Intricate, realistic cobwebs strung themselves in corners and between porch pillars. The ordinary front door transformed into one made of heavy antique wood planks reinforced with metal strips. A small window was centered over a brass gargoyle door knocker. Waiting until the two teens and their young companions reached the bottom of the porch steps, she fixed them with a solemn stare and raised her arms. "Beware!"

Hesitating, the older girl rolled her eyes. "Get real!"

Mark elbowed her again with a glance at his younger brother and sister, who stood frozen in frightened wonder. "'Come on, Lynne. The kids love this stuff."

Shrugging, the girl swept the porch with her bored, impatient gaze.

Hilda immediately put her flair for spine-tingling theater to work. The rusty hinges on the old pine coffin under the window creaked as the lid opened and a bony skeleton hand crept out.

The two children shrieked.

Lynne's dark eyes widened slightly, which Hilda recognized as a display of intense surprise for the not-easily-impressed and surly girl.

Mark jerked back, then grinned as he rested comforting hands on his brother's and sister's shoulders. "It's okay, guys. It's just a show."

With her audience hooked, Hilda snapped a warning glance at the coffin. "Get back in there, Bones. The party doesn't start till eight!"

A disappointed moan sounded as the hand retreated and the coffin lid banged closed.

"Now then." Smiling, Hilda looked at the children and clasped her hands. "Password, please."

Both children just blinked.

Mark leaned over and whispered in his sister's ear.

Swallowing hard, the little witch spoke in a barely audible rasp. "Trick-or-treat?"

"That's correct. How fortunate for you." Winking at Mark, Hilda pointed at the spider stand by the door, then moved her finger in a beckoning motion. All four kids gasped as the black stand carrying the pumpkin bowl walked across the porch on eight stiff legs.

"A remote-controlled robot?" Mark asked.

"Ask me no questions, I'll tell you no lies." Directing the stand to stop before the dumbfounded children, Hilda paused when Zelda slipped out the door, accidentally knocking the brass gargoyle, which roared.

"A door with an attitude," Lynne commented without humor. "From the ridiculous to the absurd."

"Chill," Mark said bluntly. "That's a great door."

Hilda refrained from demonstrating the real meaning of absurd by turning Lynne's perpetually peeved expression into something more suitably sour and permanent.

"Have you seen Cousin Willy, Hilda?" Zelda asked. "He was snitching Orlando's pizza squares and I told him to wait outside until everything's ready."

Glancing back, Hilda shrugged and improvised. "If he's pouting, he's probably gone into invisible mode again." As she pointed at the rocking chair, she noted that Zelda had ditched the hoopskirt in favor of a modern one that flared into flowing folds at the hips.

"Invisible mode?" Lynne repeated with sarcastic skepticism.

The chair began to rock back and forth, seemingly on its own.

"There you are, Willy." Crossing her arms, Zelda glared at the chair and casually moved a finger. "You can't possibly be starving. You're a ghost."

The chair stopped rocking as a pale mist appeared and rose off the seat. With a *whoosh,* the mist coalesced into a denser fog and swooped over the candy bowl. Snatching a Magic Munchie, it zipped through the porch railing and disappeared around the corner of the house.

Zelda sighed in resignation. "Better the treats than all that wonderful food Orlando brought in, I guess."

Nodding, Hilda eyed the astounded children and motioned toward the pumpkin bowl. "Better get yours quick before Willy comes back."

When neither child made a move to dip into the bowl, Mark picked out several pieces of candy for them. "That was drastic! How'd you do that?"

"Dry ice." Hilda waved off the compliment. "But that's nothing compared to what Sabrina's planned for the party."

"Right," Zelda agreed. "When she decides to throw a monster bash, it's a—monster bash. You're invited, aren't you?"

"Uh, yeah."

This time Lynne elbowed Mark. "We've really *got* to get going. *These* little monsters are getting tired."

"No, we're not," the tiny ghost piped up, suddenly finding his voice. "I wanna see the ghost again."

"That was just a trick," Lynne said, grabbing the kids' hands and pulling them away.

"But what a trick," Mark said as he followed them down the walk. "Best special effects I've ever seen in this neighborhood on Halloween."

Looking back over her shoulder, Lynne lowered her voice. "Those people are too weird, Mark. Just like Sabrina."

"I heard that," Salem mumbled. "Did you hear that?"

"Shhh." Zelda cupped a hand to her ear.

"So what?" Taking a deep breath, Mark shrugged. "I think everyone could be making a big mistake going to Libby's instead of coming here."

"Don't even think about it. I'm not destroying my social standing because of a bunch of stupid tricks. We're going where everyone else is going. Period." Still dragging the protesting kids, Lynne stalked into the dark.

"Maybe I should give her a fat lip," Hilda suggested as Zelda and Salem stepped up beside her.

"Buttoning her lip might be more humane," Salem said. "For everyone else."

"But it won't change her mind about which party to go to." Fuming, Zelda started to pace as Hilda pointed the spider stand to walk itself back to the door. "There's got to be something we can do. I just can't bring myself to tell Sabrina that Libby planned another party behind her back."

"Well, Mark really liked my 'special effects,'" Hilda beamed. "And the new door didn't hurt. He'd be here if that pasty-faced girlfriend of his would let him."

"And she's going to follow the crowd." Zelda frowned thoughtfully. "So we've got to get the crowd over here. I'm just not sure how."

"Maybe something like this will help." With a snap of her wrist, Hilda engraved the tombstone on top of the stack and set it beside a blazing jack-o'-lantern near the walk. Candlelight shadows danced across the crude inscription.

Monster Party in Progress. Enter If You Dare!

"As much as I hate to admit it, Hilda, it's a nice touch. We've got to start somewhere, I suppose." Nodding, Zelda brightened suddenly. "And it just may have given me another idea."

"Whatever it is, you'd better hurry. Sabrina will be home any minute."

"You stay out here in case any more of her friends stop by trick-or-treating with younger siblings," Zelda said as she turned toward the door. "Word spreads through the teenage grapevine faster than wildfire through dry brush."

"Okay. I'll make more tombstones." Hilda hesitated expectantly, then continued when Zelda didn't object. "What are you going to do?"

"I'm going to redecorate." Pausing to pat the

snarling gargoyle, Zelda looked back with a mischievous grin. "An early haunted-house motif should do nicely."

"I think so," Hilda agreed. "But how is Sabrina going to feel about it?"

"Not nearly as bad as she will if no one shows up."

Chapter 9

☆

Sabrina arrived in her room at 7:37, a few minutes after safely delivering Connie and David to their grateful father. Instantly transforming herself from a bouncy blond teenager into the intense and sultry image of Morticia Addams, she realized that Salem, who usually had no compunction about making himself at home on her bed, was nowhere to be seen. He was probably stalking Orlando's tempting cuisine, looking for an opening to snitch a tidbit without getting caught by her aunts.

That's fine with me, Sabrina thought as she studied herself in the full-length mirror. Now that the edge of her anxiety had been dulled and she was more relaxed about the impending party, she really didn't need the benefit of Salem's cynical feline opinion. Although in this case, he might actually have had something complimentary to say about the change in her appearance. There was a certain predatory intensity inherent in the Morticia look and the results were nothing short of provocative.

The floor-length black brocade dress with its daring V neck and long sleeves cuffed in ragged tatters fit her like a glove. Deciding against a wig, she had lengthened and straightened her own hair and turned it black. The new hair, combined with dark eyeliner, subtle shadows, and bright red lipstick that matched her nail polish, created a startling contrast to the pale facial makeup, giving her a deathly but attractive aura. Totally pleased with the costume, she hurried to the stairs as fast as the tight dress that hugged her legs would allow. Harvey and Jenny would be arriving any minute.

"What happened to your hoops?" Sabrina asked as she paused on the upstairs landing. Aunt Zelda's new flared skirt gave her a chic and cultured look that was infinitely more flattering than the outdated, collectible-doll representation of Glinda the old film had depicted.

"They *had* to go. I kept knocking things over." Zelda shrugged, then raised an appreciative eyebrow. "You look absolutely stunning, Sabrina."

"Enchanting." Still dressed as Merlin, but looking slightly frazzled, Aunt Hilda gave her niece an approving once-over and sighed.

"Yeah? I feel totally wicked." Quickly exchanging her girlish grin for the sly almost-smile of

Morticia, Sabrina glided down the stairs with a slow, calculated grace. When she reached the lower steps, it took a moment before her mind registered the fact that the interior of the house had been drastically altered. Not in her wildest imagination had she suspected the horror that had been wrought in her brief absence. Stumbling in shock, she grabbed the landing post to steady herself and stared in devastated disbelief.

Ambushed, Sabrina thought as she gazed at the tattered black shrouds and cobwebs hanging from the foyer ceiling and draped down the staircase railing. Her carefully selected and tastefully arranged decorations were gone, replaced by the ghastly and somber ornamentations of a third-rate nineteen-forties horror movie set. She was so dumbfounded by the realistically macabre enhancements, she could only nod in mute despair as Hilda and Zelda proudly offered to give her the grand tour through their Halloween nightmare.

"I know it's a bit overdone," Zelda apologized as her gaze swept the damp stones imbedded here and there in the walls. "But everyone who saw Hilda's props on the porch was so impressed."

"I was a hit." Bubbling with delight, Hilda raised her golden wand and struck a victorious pose.

"And after all," Zelda explained nervously, "since you're in character as Morticia, this setting is perfect. I'm absolutely positive your friends will think the house looks—"

Hilda quickly filled in the blank. "Totally awesome."

Totally gruesome, Sabrina thought as she followed her aunts through the downstairs rooms in a daze.

Thorny bushes with dry brown leaves and shriveled brown blossoms had been substituted for every thriving green plant that had graced the living room and foyer. Lichen that glowed in iridescent green clung to the window frames instead of her bright orange lights. Intricately carved jack-o'-lanterns with ferocious expressions, sleeping bats, and skulls with grotesque grins accented by twisted, leafless branches had displaced the honeycombed crepe paper pumpkins and cats and brightly colored sprigs of autumn leaves. Lights dimmed to shine at a maximum output of twenty-five watts augmented by dozens of strategically placed, flickering candles further enhanced the dark and gloomy atmosphere.

But that was not the worst of it, Sabrina realized as her numbed senses slowly returned to normal. A life-size skeleton wearing a top hat and tails was seated at the piano. The ivory keys depressed and rose as unseen fingers played a minor-key dirge that could just barely be heard.

"I know your friends are probably too old to take bobbing for apples seriously, but I bet they'll get a kick out of this anyway." Aunt Zelda pointed to a half barrel made of wooden staves bound together with metal.

Prepared for anything, Sabrina cautiously peered at two dozen apples floating in the water. A white skull popped up suddenly, then slowly submerged again. She hoped none of her guests had weak hearts.

"And you'll never guess what's in here!"

Afraid to ask, Sabrina just looked at Hilda, who flung open the door of an ornately carved but dingy coffin standing upright in a corner.

"Ta-dah! The phone!"

"Really?" Coughing, Sabrina waved away a cloud of dust released from the old coffin. She could just see Libby or one of the cheerleader's fastidious friends using the old-fashioned hand-crank phone hanging on the inside to call the local newspaper to report that a family of demented and dangerous weirdos had invaded the community. The only thing missing in the morbid setting was a foggy mist rising from the moss-covered carpet.

Ducking to avoid being dive-bombed by a screeching bat whose slumber was disturbed when Aunt Hilda slammed the coffin closed, Sabrina asked, "What about the food?"

"Fantastic!" Aunt Zelda motioned her to follow as she headed for the dining-room door. "Orlando is an arrogant pain in the butt, but he does live up to his reputation. Your guests will not go hungry."

If any of them makes it as far as the dining room, Sabrina thought glumly as she started through the doorway.

"Oops. I almost forgot." Pausing behind her, Aunt Hilda executed a casual point. A mist immediately began to rise. "No authentic haunted house is complete without a foggy mist swirling around the floor."

Accepting the mist as inconsequential given the overall disaster, Sabrina asked warily, "What do you mean by *authentic* haunted house?"

Aunt Hilda glowed. "Willy was such a hit with the trick-or-treaters, I thought he should stick around."

"Are you telling me there's a real ghost? In this house?"

"No!" Scoffing, Hilda waved her concerns aside. "He's just a little guy I conjured up that swoops in and out snatching food."

"Oh, well. That makes all the difference." Letting Aunt Hilda go into the dining room first, Sabrina looked up as an eerie, muted howl sounded from above.

Hilda glanced back. "Don't worry about him."

"What is him—I mean, he? It?"

"I'm not exactly sure." Hilda shrugged. "I think he came with the castle stones Zelda imported from Romania, but I'm pretty sure he can't get out of the bathroom."

Sabrina shuddered. All of a sudden, the prospect

that no one would come to the party didn't seem nearly so awful.

Pausing as Hilda ducked through the dining-room doorway, Sabrina thought about just changing everything back with a simple flick of her finger, then realized she couldn't change her aunts' spells. Somehow, she had to convince *them* to reinstate her original decorations—without hurting their feelings. And she had only about two minutes left to do it. She would just have to be firm. Bracing herself, she followed Hilda into the dining room.

"Listen, I know you both went to a lot of trouble—" Sabrina held back her request when she realized her aunts were too preoccupied to listen.

Standing in the nearest corner looking over Zelda's shoulder, Hilda inhaled a pungent cinnamon-laced aroma. "Smells wonderful, but how does it taste?"

Sabrina flinched as Zelda stopped stirring the smoking green concoction bubbling in a huge cauldron and ladled out a dipperful for Hilda. At least the big black pot wasn't in the living room.

Sipping, frowning, then nodding, Hilda handed the ladle back. "That could be the best batch of Hocus-pocus Punch you've ever made."

Zelda rubbed her chin thoughtfully. "I think it needs more nutmeg. Where's Salem? He's the expert."

A soft mew drew Sabrina's appalled attention to the large dining table, and once again she was stricken speechless with surprise. The table was draped with the ordinary white paper tablecloth boasting a winsome jack-o'-lantern and green vine design that she had chosen from Orlando's holiday selection. More important, the standard bowls, platters, and warmers were heaped with all the finger foods, snacks, and sandwich makings she had ordered. She wasn't quite sure what she had expected after seeing her aunts' other horrendous innovations. Fried newts wrapped in bats' wings? Sheep's eyes sautéed in snake oil? Or, perhaps, alligator on a stick spiced with Amazon fungus pepper?

Instead, plates of Halloween cookies, chips, dips, crackers, cheeses, chocolates, and nuts sat on one end of the long table. Platters of cold cuts and sliced cheese and a variety of breads and sandwich spreads were artistically arranged on the far end. Lifting off the tops of the warmers in the middle, Sabrina was delighted to see hot pizza squares, spicy chicken wings, meatballs in a tangy sauce, mini–hot dogs, and small shrimp egg rolls. Paper plates, napkins, and plastic cups in the same pattern as the tablecloth and plastic forks were neatly stacked in front of the warmers. Orlando had done everything to her exact specifications—except for the centerpiece. She had picked out a fake jack-o'-lantern with trailing green vines to match the paper products. Instead, he had brought—

"Salem!"

Back hunched with a shrimp egg roll clamped in his jaws, the cat hung his head. He had obviously been on the table helping himself to the goodies when Aunt Zelda had walked in and surprised him. In self-defense, he had assumed the temporary role of centerpiece on the off chance that no one would notice.

Biting off the end of the small egg roll, Salem looked up as he chewed, then swallowed. "And that completes my inspection, Sabrina. The egg rolls are perfectly safe to eat."

Fuming, Sabrina tapped her foot. "Where's the real centerpiece?"

"You mean that Styrofoam thing with the phony smile and oversize teeth?" Salem's tail twitched as he glanced over the back edge of the table. "On the floor."

"Which is where *you* belong! Scat!" Shooing the cat off the table with a wave of her wand, Hilda eyed Orlando's spread with a hungry gleam. Stabbing a meatball with a plastic fork, she chewed and nodded. "These are safe, too."

Grinning, Sabrina pointed the pumpkin centerpiece back onto the table and began arranging the long green vines around the warmers. She jumped when the doorbell rang. "That must be Harvey and Jenny!"

"Don't bother," Hilda said. "The butler will get it."

"Butler?" Sabrina frowned. "What butler?"

A high-pitched, chilling scream reverberated through the house.

Hitching up her tight skirt, Sabrina bolted through the door and skidded to a halt when she saw what was happening in the foyer.

A huge man who looked remarkably like Lurch was holding the door open for Harvey and Jenny, who were both staring at him in terrified awe.

Hilda smiled tightly as she stepped up beside her stunned niece. "That butler."

☆

Chapter 10

☆

You hired somebody who looks like Lurch to answer the door?" Sabrina laughed. "Cool!"

"Hired? Not exactly," Hilda admitted. "His name is Stagger."

Zelda appeared on Sabrina's other side. "A close approximation of the Addams Family butler, but not. Like your Roller Blahs."

Sabrina didn't appreciate being reminded of the in-line skates she had acquired with her magic and then was too embarrassed to use because of the hideous name. However, as she watched Harvey and Jenny recover from their shock, she decided that in this case, using a close copy with a different name really didn't matter. Having a butler who resembled the infamous Lurch answer the door for the party was almost as good as having Orlando cater it.

With a subtle nod and a blank, enigmatic

expression on his gaunt face, Stagger stood back to let Sabrina's first two guests enter.

"See," Hilda said. "Stagger doesn't have even a hint of a smile like that other guy."

After she cautiously eased by the giant man, Jenny rushed up to Sabrina. The tambourine tied to her red sash jingled with the rhythm of her movements. "That guy is great! And I can't believe what you did to your house!"

Turning back toward the kitchen, Zelda grabbed Hilda's arm and dragged her along. However, they hovered in the doorway, burning with curiosity.

"Yeah, neither can I," Sabrina mumbled as Jenny gaped about her in wide-eyed wonder and tossed back a wild mass of long crimped hair. The big gold hoops in her ears and bunches of bangles on her arm added a touch of daring to the simple peasant blouse, long skirt, and high-laced boots that constituted her *Wolfman* gypsy outfit. Like Stagger, she fit right in with the vintage horror movie ambiance Hilda and Zelda had achieved.

"It's *totally* awesome."

Sabrina sensed her aunts' totally pleased reaction to Jenny's critique of their handiwork. So maybe she *had* overreacted and the realistic haunted-house decor *wasn't* a total catastrophe. Still, her best friend's preferences and quirks in everything from music to books to movies and clothes was slightly askew of the norm, so Jenny's opinion didn't necessarily reflect the results of a popular poll. However, since it was too late to change things back now that Jenny and Harvey had arrived, Sabrina wisely opted to make the best of it.

"And that costume!" Taking a step backward, Jenny exhaled with admiration. "It's so—so—"

"Ravishing." Harvey's soft-spoken voice resonated with a seductive timbre that was completely out of character for him, but suited Gomez Addams's roguishly suave demeanor.

Sabrina's heart turned somersaults when she looked up and saw him lounging against the doorjamb separating the foyer and the living room. Wearing the vertically striped suit, white shirt, black silk tie, and black boots she had provided, he looked as dashing and dangerous as the playful leer he bestowed upon her. Never dreaming that her sweet and charmingly naive Harvey would dive into his role as Gomez Addams with such romantic abandon, she watched in breathless anticipation as he ambled toward her.

Equally captivated by the unexpected change in Harvey's persona, Jenny and her aunts vicariously experienced similar heart-stopping responses when he paused before her and held her entranced gaze with intense brown eyes.

"You look absolutely wretched tonight, Tish."

Having rented and watched the Addams Family movies half a dozen times since deciding on her costume, Sabrina had no trouble picking up her cue as Morticia. Dcspite the lack of oxygen in her lungs, she managed to mimic the sensuous character's coldly passionate voice.

"Oh, Gomez. You say the most horrible things."

"Cara mia—" Without warning, Harvey swept Sabrina into his arms, dipped her backward with the obvious intention of kissing her—and almost dropped her when Aunt Zelda loudly interrupted.

"Has anyone seen my star wand?"

Jolted back to reality and suddenly realizing he had the rapt and undivided attention of an audience, Harvey fumbled the precarious embrace and blushed.

"I think I left it over there."

Struggling to stay on her feet as Harvey let go of her, Sabrina staggered back into an upright position as Aunt Zelda drove a wedge between them to retrieve the wand from the coffee table where—she was certain—it had not been a moment before.

"Sorry." Smiling as though she had not just ruined one of Sabrina's most perfect, never-to-be-repeated moments in life, Zelda raised the wand. The number-one hit on the current alternative music charts immediately wafted through hidden speakers at a decibel level significantly below deafening. Then she waved Hilda into the dining room and scurried after her. "Have fun!"

I was, Sabrina fumed.

"Who is she supposed to be?" Harvey asked, recovering his normal voice and trying to recover his dignity.

"Glinda, the Good Witch of the North." Sabrina scowled. "But apparently she's a little confused, because she's acting like the Wicked Witch of the East."

"Don't blame her, Sabrina. I got a little carried away myself." Grinning sheepishly, Harvey glanced around the room. "Besides, anyone who would trash their house for a Halloween party *can't* be bad."

"You're right." Sighing, Sabrina smiled with chagrin and relief. Things were going much better than she had dared hope, and she found herself slipping into the macabre spirit of the night.

"All this stuff looks so real!" Jenny exclaimed.

Leaning over to inspect an arrangement of dry bell-shaped flowers surrounded by prickly leaves on thorny stems sitting on the baby grand piano, Harvey jerked back. "That flower just tried to bite me!"

Rolling her eyes, Sabrina shook her head in mock disgust. "Aunt Hilda must have forgotten to feed it again."

Staring at the skeleton seated on the piano bench, Jenny jumped with a soft cry of alarm as the bony figure's head dropped and turned slightly to stare back through dark, empty eye sockets.

"Don't mind him, Jenny." Sounding as casual about such strange occurrences as her Aunt Hilda, Sabrina added, "He was a typical lounge lizard when he was alive, too."

"Lounge lizard?"

"Cocktail bar piano player with a line as smooth as his voice and an eye for the ladies," Sabrina explained.

"Oh." Still puzzled, Jenny grinned as Stagger entered carrying a tray of cups filled with green punch that were still smoking. When everyone had helped themselves and the hulking butler mutely excused himself with a sedate bow, she bubbled over with an enthusiasm that was seconded by the gurgling punch.

"This isn't going to be the party of the year, Sabrina. It's going to be the bash of the century! Libby will absolutely *bust* with envy."

Casting a look at an ornate wall clock that marked the passing seconds with the sound of a thudding heartbeat and began to bong the hour, Sabrina crossed her fingers and glanced at the front door where Stagger waited in silent and immobile patience. Except for Harvey and Jenny, who had been invited to come by ahead of schedule, no one had arrived early.

Twenty minutes later, Sabrina began to fret. Harvey and Jenny were sampling the food, and except for a couple of last-minute trick-or-treaters Stagger had sent screaming for their lives when he opened the door, the doorbell hadn't rung. Either everyone had decided to be fashionably late—not likely—or no one was coming.

"I can't stand this, Zelda." Returning to the kitchen after sneaking another peek into the living room, Hilda paced in furious agitation.

Pointing at an empty pot, Zelda conjured another batch of meatballs and took a tentative taste.

"Close?" Hilda asked hopefully. Zelda was trying to duplicate Orlando's recipes to ensure that the food didn't run out. Although at the moment it didn't look like that would be a problem.

"Exact." Pointing the meatballs out of existence until needed, Zelda sat down. "So what are they doing?"

"Watching Salem watch the apple tub waiting for the skull to surface again. I added a shriek to liven things up a little, but I doubt that it'll help Sabrina's sagging spirits much." Heaving a distressed sigh, Hilda fell into another chair and conjured a steaming cup of coffee. "This is all that Libby's fault."

"Hmmm. Planning another party behind Sabrina's back was pretty low," Zelda agreed. "Even for her."

"Well, I can play that game, too." Setting her

cup down, Hilda shrugged the cloak back over her shoulders, straightened her pointed hat, and pushed up the sleeves of her tunic.

"What are you doing?" Zelda asked.

"Simple. Sabrina's wondering where all her guests are, right? Well, I'm going to arrange it so Libby's wondering where all her guests *went!*"

Clamping her hand around Hilda's arm as she raised it, Zelda narrowed her eyes in warning. "As much as I'd like to just zap all those kids out of Libby's house and deposit them over here, we can't. People, including the police, are much too susceptible to believing weird stories about impossible incidents on Halloween, and a stunt like that would attract too much attention."

"There's no such thing as too much attention." Arriving in a swirl of pink smoke to the sound of a drumroll, Aunt Vesta materialized by the back door wearing an elegant blue-sequined evening gown and a sparkling feather boa.

"Hello, Vesta," Zelda said with an enthusiasm that would bore a mushroom to death.

"What are you doing here?" Hilda asked bluntly. Their ordinary suburban kitchen was the last place she expected to find their flamboyant and irresponsible other sister on this particular night. Although she lived almost exclusively in the Other Realm, Vesta couldn't resist using her magic to taunt and torment the blue-blooded upper echelons of New England society on Halloween in reprisal for crimes committed against witches by their illustrious ancestors.

"I knew I'd find you both here doing nothing tonight." Dropping the boa, Vesta sank into a comfortable wingback chair that appeared with a snap of her fingers.

"And what made you so certain we'd be home?" Hilda challenged.

"Cousin Marigold canceled her traditional dinner. Where else would you be?" Raising a mischievous eyebrow, Vesta smiled slyly. "I thought you might want to go out for a little nasty but bloodless adult trick-or-treating for a change. I'm meeting some friends you might find rather intriguing."

"No, thanks. We'll stay home," Hilda said, bristling at the implied insult. "But we're not doing nothing."

"Quite the contrary." Peering at Vesta with bold annoyance, Zelda explained. "Sabrina's worst nightmare has come true, I'm afraid."

"Don't tell me she lost her powers?" Vesta's perfectly manicured hand flew to her mouth. "Or did that dreadful Drell banish her because she's half mortal?"

"No," Zelda said patiently. "She's having a Halloween party—and no one came."

"Almost no one," Hilda corrected. "Harvey and Jenny are here."

"The best friend and boyfriend." Vesta nodded.

"I remember seeing them on Super Secret Inside-a-Vision when Sabrina visited me in the Pleasure Dome. Cute, but dull, as I recall."

"We like them." Hilda smiled through gritted teeth.

"No doubt. So—" Crossing her long legs, Vesta shifted her questioning glance between them. "What's the problem?"

"We just told you," Hilda hissed in exasperation. "No one came to the party!"

"Is that all?" Dismissing the problem and the wingback chair, Vesta smiled. "That's *not* a problem."

Hilda frowned as Vesta popped out with a suspicious lack of fanfare. "What's she up to?"

"Making life miserable for a few deserving politicians, probably." Zelda sighed, too focused on Sabrina to worry about Vesta's plans for the evening. "You know, I don't think Harvey and Jenny knew about Libby's party, either, or they would have said something."

"I agree." Taking off her wizard's hat, Hilda fluffed her matted hair.

"Do you have any regular mustard?" Jenny asked, sticking her head inside the door.

"Yes. Help yourself." Zelda gestured toward the refrigerator, then looked up sharply. "But first, come sit down for a minute, will you?"

"Sure." Shrugging uncertainly, Jenny perched on the edge of her seat. "Is something wrong?"

"Very wrong." Hilda wasn't quite sure what

Zelda was hoping to accomplish with Jenny, but facts were facts. "Don't you think it's kind of strange that it's eight-thirty and none of your friends have shown up yet? Except you and Harvey, of course."

"Yeah, but I didn't want to rub Sabrina's nose in it." Frowning, Jenny shifted uncomfortably. "She's been a nervous wreck ever since you gave her permission to have this party. I mean, I'm not exactly plugged into the social grapevine, but I honestly didn't expect *everyone* would snub her. Especially since there's nothing else going on except a freshman dance."

"Wrong. Libby's having a party, too," Hilda blurted out. "Everyone's there."

"No way!"

"Way." Zelda nodded. "We overheard a couple of your friends talking about going to a party at Libby's when they came by trick-or-treating earlier."

Jenny sat back, her eyes flashing with outrage. "Everyone we *know* must have been in on the secret, and not one single person said a word! But you know what? They're the ones who are really losing out. I mean, being greeted by that Stagger character at the door was just too cool. Between him and Orlando's food and the way you've done the house, this party could have been totally—"

"Awesome," the aunts said in unison.

"Totally." Jenny sighed.

"Too bad no one knows about it," Zelda hinted.

"Too true," Jenny agreed. "They'd leave Libby's and flock here like locusts swarming over a few hundred miles of choice farmland."

"If they knew about it," Hilda pressed, finally tuning into Zelda's plan and hoping the girl had gotten the message. She caught Zelda's eye and shrugged as Jenny stared into space for several long seconds. She really didn't want to resort to stronger methods of persuasion.

"I don't suppose you have Libby's phone number?" Jenny asked suddenly.

"Now that you mention it—" Zelda flicked her finger toward the counter on the far side of the central island. "It's on that piece of paper over there."

As Jenny got up and moved across the kitchen, Hilda was struck with another inspired idea. Since Stagger had made such a great impression, a few more uninvited but interesting guests whose public-domain status didn't require them to be close copies like the butler couldn't hurt. Willy was cute but too tame for the teenaged crowd they hoped to attract. Flicking her finger, she tensed as Jenny rounded the end of the island, stopped, turned white, and shrieked.

"What?" Zelda jumped up in a panic, then saw Hilda's wink and slumped.

"There's a—a mummy lying on your kitchen floor!"

"On the floor? In here?" Zelda huffed with

displeasure. "The mummy is not supposed to be in the kitchen, Hilda."

"I know, I know." Scurrying around the other end of the counter, Hilda leaned over the prone and slightly crumbling mummy she had conjured, and shook an angry finger in his bandaged face. "I told you to wait in the den."

Nodding stiffly, the mummy tried to pull himself up into a sitting position but couldn't. His legs were bound together and his arms were wrapped against his body, giving him the appearance of a gigantic cocoon.

"Frank!" Hilda yelled with another deft point.

Jenny giggled in pure delight as Frankenstein's monster pounded on, then broke down, the back door.

Quickly casting a spell to muffle the crash, Hilda smiled as Dr. Frankenstein's creation lumbered over. "Would you mind helping this decaying gentleman into the den?"

Grunting in the traditionally limited vocabulary of most low-budget movie monsters, the massive man with bolts in his neck, a plastic flattop, cross-stitched scars, and ragged clothes picked up the mummy, flung him over his shoulder, and walked out through the dining room.

"Where did you find these guys?" Jenny asked. "They are *really* good."

Pleased with Jenny's astonished reaction to her latest trick, and batting a thousand, Hilda shrugged. "They're listed in your local *TV Guide.*"

"Yeah, right. Where's the phone? It would be just too cruel not to let *somebody* know what's going on here."

"You can use the cordless over there," Hilda suggested. "It's so dusty in the phone coffin, you wouldn't be able to talk without sneezing after every other word."

"Uh, okay. Thanks." Grabbing the phone, Jenny carefully skirted the downed back door to go outside for quiet and privacy.

"Are we brilliant or what?" Giving Zelda a thumbs-up, Hilda went back to the table to get her hat and grinned as Sabrina's startled scream rose from the living room.

"What's that all about?" Zelda asked.

"I think it's safe to assume another delightfully terrifying star of movie monsterdom just showed up at the front door."

Zelda frowned. "I'm not so sure this motley menagerie was such a good idea. At least Stagger has manners. What if these creatures don't behave themselves?"

Pulling on her hat, Hilda shook her golden wand. "If they cause any trouble, I'll send them back to celluloid limbo where they came from. But don't worry. I've impressed the absolute necessity of practicing safe scares in their deranged minds. I don't think they'll get out of control."

"But we will!" Still wearing her elegant evening gown and boa, Vesta popped back to the sound of trumpets.

Hilda and Zelda gawked in horrified surprise as two other witches and a handsome young warlock popped in after her.

"It's party time," Vesta announced with an impish grin that made Hilda wilt in helpless dismay.

☆

Chapter 11

☆

Okay! What's going on?" Sabrina barged into the kitchen babbling and close to hysteria. "Frankenstein's monster is walking around with an unraveling mummy slung over his shoulder. A glob of pulsing rubbery stuff has taken up residence in the coffin with the phone, and some weird scaly guy with webbed feet is sitting in the guest bathroom sink!"

"You noticed." Hilda winced.

"She's not blind," Zelda muttered with an annoyed point at the door lying on the floor. Righting itself, the door shot back into its proper opening. Another point remounted the hinges torn from the doorjamb and replaced the splintered wood around the latch bolt.

"They're not exactly easy to ignore." Calming down a little, Sabrina took a deep breath, then realized her aunts were not alone in the kitchen. "Aunt Vesta!"

"My! Don't you look wickedly glamorous tonight, Sabrina."

"Thanks. What are you doing here?"

"I heard you were having a party and thought I'd drop by with a few friends." The boa slipped off one shoulder as Vesta gestured toward the three people standing behind her. "I've known Helena for more than a hundred and seventy-five years. Ever since we both tried to short-sheet Napoleon's cot the night before he was soundly thrashed by Wellington at the Battle of Waterloo."

"He deserved it, the two-timing runt."

Sabrina flinched as the tall, slim woman wearing a slinky crimson red gown picked a compact out of thin air and checked her makeup.

Turning to the short, decidedly plump woman on her other side, Vesta sighed. "And Catherine's psychologist has prescribed spending Halloween with me until her suppressed sense of humor is awakened. Last year she actually smiled."

Catherine had dark hair pulled back and twisted into a severe bun that emphasized her dour expression. Wearing a frumpy sweater, baggy blouse and skirt, and clunky old-lady shoes, she clutched a handbag in front of her and harrumphed in obvious irritation.

"And Rafe is my protégé," Vesta concluded. "He's also quite cute, don't you think?"

The gorgeous young man in the exquisitely

tailored tuxedo executed a sweeping bow. "Your humble servant, Lady Sabrina. Vesta's glowing words of praise dim in the brilliance of your enchanting presence."

"Thanks. I think." Remembering her aunts' concerns about the tendency of some witches and warlocks to disregard professional prudence for the sake of fun at mortal expense on Halloween, an inclination that definitely included her irrepressible Aunt Vesta, Sabrina shot Hilda and Zelda a desperate glance.

"Don't look at us. *We* didn't invite her!" Hilda's pointed hat tilted as she folded her arms and flounced in a minifit of temper.

"This is a party for Sabrina's school friends, Vesta," Zelda said gently.

"Speaking of friends, where's Jenny?" Sabrina's voice cracked as she glanced around the room and realized that her best friend wasn't there. "All she wanted was a little mustard."

"Jenny's on the phone," Zelda assured her. "Outside."

Noting that the cordless phone *was* missing from the base, Sabrina sagged as Vesta waved off Zelda's futile attempt to discourage her from crashing the party.

"I'm sure a few extra guests won't make any difference. Sabrina doesn't mind, do you, dear?"

"No, but—" As much as Sabrina adored her other aunt, she knew Vesta could not be trusted to contain her exuberant predilection to overwhelm and victimize mortals with her magic. Shaking off another panic attack, Sabrina grasped at the only reason she could think of why Vesta and company shouldn't stay. "The theme is monster movies and you're not in costume."

"Easily fixed." With a casual flip of her wrist, Vesta transformed herself into a sleek and snarling facsimile of Cat Woman.

"Pretend to be someone else?" Rafe blinked dark eyes framed in magnificently long and lush lashes. "What a charming concept." Snapping his fingers, he added tails, a silver-knobbed cane, and a red-lined black cape to his tux. Smoothing back his thick black hair and elongating his gleaming white canine teeth into fangs, he became a very real warlock posing as a vampire.

"Or something else." Vesta's finger shot out.

A confused frown darkened the alabaster sheen of Helena's flawless complexion as she suddenly ballooned into the shape of a giant tomato still sporting its capped stem.

"Oh, dear. That's not *exactly* what I had in mind." Vesta pointed again, restoring Helena to her original form covered by the daring red dress. However, a wide-brimmed green hat shaped like the jagged cap and stem of a tomato crowned her short dark hair.

"Killer," Sabrina quipped.

"Don't even think about turning *me* into some kind of monster, Vesta," Catherine the Cranky warned.

"Not at all *necessary,"* Vesta parried.

Frowning as the insult zipped over her head, Catherine harrumphed.

Sabrina graciously surrendered to the inevitable. Aunt Vesta would not take no for an answer. However, since no one but her two closest friends had come to the party, it hardly mattered.

Nobody but Sabrina noticed when Jenny opened the door and paused in transfixed astonishment, obviously wondering how it had been fixed so quickly. Darting back inside as though she was leaping through a portal of fire, she closed it with great care and scurried behind the group of costumed strangers to hang the phone on its base. Sabrina decided not to even attempt an explanation.

"Hey, Sabrina!" Harvey dashed through the door. "Have you got any smelling salts?"

"What for?" Sabrina gasped in alarm.

"Casey Hill and Lauren Wentworth just fainted on the porch. I guess coming face-to-face with a roaring brass gargoyle was a little too much for them."

"Ohmigosh!" Sabrina paled as Hilda discreetly pointed up the needed stimulant and handed it to her. "Are they hurt?"

"Naw." Harvey stuffed one hand in his trouser pocket and thumbed over his shoulder with the other. "Brent Jeffers and Terry Pringle broke their fall."

"Brent and Terry?" Sabrina started as the meaning of Harvey's words slowly sank in. "You mean they're here? At the party?"

"Not quite. They're still on the porch, but Ned Wallace is in the living room taking notes for an article in the school paper. I think he's really impressed."

"Wahoo!" Fisting the smelling salts, Sabrina grabbed Jenny's arm and hauled her out of the kitchen.

Lying on the sideboard in the dining room, tail twitching and drooling over the shrimp egg rolls on the table, a guilty-looking Salem shrunk back as Sabrina dashed in, then perked up when she ran by him without a word. She no longer cared if the cat helped himself to a tender morsel or two. There were people at the door.

When they hit the living room, Brent and Terry were helping the dazed Casey and Lauren stumble to the couch. Harvey took the smelling salts and went to assist.

Ned, who was wearing black jeans and a dark long-sleeve shirt with his white Michael Myers mask hanging around his neck, was checking under the piano, apparently looking for the self-play mechanism or computer control that didn't exist. The ivory keys were pounding out another gloomy dirge that added an oddly harmonic base-line to the alternative song coming through the speakers.

"Hey, Sabrina. Jenny." Ned, a tall and lanky basketball player, bonked his head on the underside of the piano trying to stand up, then rubbed the spot as he moved out from under it more cautiously. "Sorry I was late. I, uh—had some things to do."

"No problem!" Sabrina beamed brightly. "Better late than not at all."

"I'll say. I have never seen anything like this! The fun house at Zillions of Thrills is a kiddy ride by comparison."

"Whoa. Far out!"

Sabrina looked toward the foyer where the towering butler stood holding the door open as more teens wandered in in pairs or by themselves. Costumed as everyone from the horrific Elm Street nightmare, Freddie Krueger, to zombies in various stages of decay, wounded victims in torn, dirty clothes, and witches, vampires, and werewolves that ranged from ludicrous to grotesque to elegantly chic, the guests entered to peer about the grim and gruesome surroundings without regard to maintaining their normally impossible-to-shake cool. On Aunt Hilda's astounded-delight scale, the average reaction rated a ten.

"You look great, Sabrina." The grosser-than-average zombie grinned and gave her an admiring nod, arousing the undisguised ire of his pale-faced companion.

"Thanks, Mark. Hi, Lynne."

Setting her glossed lips in an angry pout, Lynne dragged her boyfriend away with her nose firmly planted in the air.

"What's her problem?" Sabrina asked Jenny. She barely knew Lynne and didn't recall ever doing anything to her that warranted such blatant hostility.

"Who cares?" Jenny shrugged with a mysterious smile teasing the corners of her mouth. "I never did like her."

A series of gasps and startled cries rippled through the crowd gathering in the living room as the Frankenstein monster walked through carrying a paper plate heaped with cheese squares, meatballs, and chicken wings.

"Hey, buddy!" The unidentified boy dressed as Freddie craned his neck to look up into the monster's pasty green face. "Where'd you get that food?"

Grunting, the monster pointed toward the dining-room door and popped a hot dog in his mouth. As he continued on his stiff-legged, lumbering way, Sabrina noticed Salem trotting close behind, scarfing up the tidbits the clumsy monster dropped.

Wondering where he had ditched the mummy, Sabrina decided to mingle and look for the preserved corpse at the same time. As she turned away from the piano, another startled shriek drew her attention to the phone coffin.

"Something slimy stole the egg roll right out of my hand!" Tracey Lopez, barefooted, wearing a high-necked, long-sleeved gothic nightgown with a shawl draped over her shoulders, and carrying a brass candlestick, screamed again. "Oh, gross. It just slid over my feet!"

Great, Sabrina thought as she made a beeline for the coffin and looked inside. The blob was gone; present location unknown.

"I think I'm going to be sick." Tracey gagged.

Jumping up from the couch, Harvey grabbed a bowl from the coffee table, dumped the peanuts on the floor, and handed it to the nauseated girl. Then he nodded toward the den beyond the foyer. "The bathroom's over there."

Dropping her candlestick and clutching the bowl to her chest, the gothic damsel in distress ran.

A disgusting slurping noise came from under the coffee table followed by a satisfied belch.

"What was that?" Casey cried in alarm.

"I don't know." Brent shrugged. "But all the peanuts are gone."

Grateful for the dim lighting that prevented anyone from actually seeing the blob in action, and hoping it would take an after-snack nap in some secluded corner, Sabrina chased Tracey.

"Wait!" Catching up, Sabrina grabbed the girl by the shoulders and aimed her at the stairs. After her too-close encounter with a slimy lump of ravenous protoplasm, the girl's sanity certainly wouldn't survive a face-to-face meeting with the Creature from the Black Lagoon monopolizing the guest bathroom sink. Or the unknown, howling something from Romania Aunt Zelda had trapped in the upstairs bathroom, either. Spinning the gagging girl around again, Sabrina gratefully handed her over to Jenny, who propelled her into the kitchen. The retching sounds she heard a moment later were drowned out by the gargoyle's vicious roar.

Since Stagger had abandoned his post for reasons unknown and which she preferred not to question, Sabrina answered the door and froze.

Poised on the porch, Bela Lugosi's infamous version of Count Dracula stared back with his overly dramatic, intense, and riveting gaze. "Good evening."

Slamming the door closed in his face, Sabrina leaned against it and took a deep breath. Except for Tracey, no one seemed particularly upset, surprised, or grossed out by the notorious film monsters Aunt Hilda had managed to conjure. Probably because they assumed the creatures were being portrayed by real people. Even so, the blob was on an eating binge. The mummy was missing. Both bathrooms were occupied and unavailable, and it was only just past nine.

Dracula was definitely overkill.

Hearing the jingle of Jenny's tambourine,

Sabrina looked up as the girl wandered out of the kitchen, staring at her open hand with a confused frown.

"What's that?" Glancing back as she stepped away from the door, Sabrina saw Dracula pressing his face against the small window to peer in, and quickly steered Jenny off to the side. If the Count didn't go away soon, she'd let Stagger handle him—if and when he returned.

"It's a silver bullet. Some creepy old guy named Larry gave it to me." Shuddering, Jenny dropped the bullet in the pot of dried thornbushes on the high chest by the door.

"Did he have an unusually hairy face?" Since no Halloween party with real movie monsters would be complete without the Wolfman, and if nothing else Aunt Hilda was thorough, Sabrina was pretty sure Jenny's creepy old guy was Larry Talbot, the unfortunate victim of the werewolf's bite. In the movie, the gypsy girl had ended his misery by shooting him with a silver bullet. But no matter what else happened, she was *not* going to allow that event to repeat itself at her party!

"No, but he did look vaguely familiar."

When the gargoyle roared again, Jenny threw open the door before Sabrina could stop her. However, it wasn't the Count. Dressed as Herman and Lily Munster, Richard Bailey and Sarah Payne rushed in.

"*That* is truly radical." Richard reached out to

touch the gargoyle and quickly yanked his hand back when it snarled.

"Will you look at this place!" Sarah gaped, wide-eyed and openmouthed as Vesta the Cat Woman cruised by with Mark on her arm.

Separating from Jenny and the Munsters, Sabrina hissed, "What happened to Lynne, Aunt Vesta?"

"The girlfriend? She jilted this poor boy to make a play for Rafe."

"Promise me you'll behave yourself," Sabrina pleaded.

"We're just going to watch some Inside-a-Vision," Aunt Vesta insisted with a hurt look as she led the miserable zombie away. "You're probably well rid of that fickle little vixen, Mark. Besides, Rafe prefers to be the pursuer. She doesn't stand a chance. You'll see."

Rolling her eyes, Sabrina was rudely intercepted as she started back toward Jenny and her friends.

"Where's the ladies room?" a scowling Catherine demanded.

"That way." Deadpan, Sabrina pointed toward the downstairs guest bathroom where the amphibious creature was hanging out, and smiled as the dowdy little witch tucked her purse under her arm and waddled away.

"We owe you one for this, Jenny." Richard put an affectionate arm around Sarah's shoulders.

"For what?" Sabrina asked, coming in on the end of the conversation.

"For calling Ned Wallace over at Libby's to tell him what a fantastic party we were missing." Sarah grinned. "Mark was so blown away by your aunt's tricks when he was here earlier, we decided we'd better check it out."

"Libby's?" Sabrina frowned.

"And if the rest of the gang doesn't get here soon," Richard said, "*we'll* call to let them know that Jenny was not joking."

"What were you doing at Libby's?"

Richard and Sarah stopped grinning and exchanged uncomfortable glances.

"Libby decided to have a party, too," Jenny explained.

"A surprise birthday party for Brad Shaefer," Sarah added quickly. "She swore everyone to secrecy and told us if we breathed a word of it to anyone and spoiled the surprise, we'd be sorry."

"It never occurred to us that you and Harvey and Jenny didn't know about it." Richard sighed.

"*I* can't believe Libby set us up and we fell for it," Sarah seethed. "The rat."

"Doesn't matter much now, though, does it?" Jenny smiled as her gaze swept the mob of kids checking out the bizarre decorations, munching Orlando's snacks, dancing in a crowded corner, and sitting around talking and laughing.

"No," Sabrina agreed with a satisfied smile. "It certainly doesn't."

Amused shrieks and laughter rose from the den as the web-footed water creature ran squealing in panic through the foyer and into the living room with Catherine hot on his flat heels, pounding him with her handbag.

"Don't you 'sweetie' me, frogface!"

Almost doubling over, Jenny wrapped her arms around her stomach and laughed until her eyes watered.

Sabrina sighed, relieved that at least one bathroom was now monster-free.

"Too bad Libby isn't here," Sarah observed smugly. "This party is so ragin', she'd be absolutely livid."

"Careful, Libby," Cee Cee warned with a worried frown. "If you don't get a grip, you'll have a nervous breakdown right here on the spot!"

"Don't tell me what to do!" Eyes gleaming with fury, Libby glared at Cee Cee, who was dressed in weird but hot clothes like any one of several teen witches in a dozen different movies. Then she turned her blazing gaze on the deserted living room as the CD playing on the stereo came to an abrupt end, casting a pall of silence over the mess her vanishing guests had left behind.

Paper plates, crumbled chips, and half-filled cups littered the floor and tables, and the ends of several orange streamers she had hastily put up dangled from the ceiling. She had not gone to too much trouble or wasted time decorating, and she had deliberately limited herself to ordinary snacks to prove that she could subvert Sabrina's party on the basis of nothing but her own reputation and social standing. And it had worked! Not even the tantalizing prospect of food by Orlando had been worth taking the risk of offending her. Everyone she had invited had shown up at her house instead of going to the Spellmans'.

Until about half an hour ago when the crowd had suddenly started to thin.

Cee Cee picked up a torn honeycombed pumpkin Brad Shaefer had been using to demonstrate his football passing technique, and sighed. The birthday boy was as painfully absent as everyone else. "So where did they go?"

Wearing her cheerleading uniform, Jill just shrugged and tugged nervously on one of her blond ponytails.

"Just guess!" Setting her jaw, Libby whirled when she heard the bathroom door open and spotted Gordie, a geek who had infiltrated the elite assemblage by dressing as the nerd turned cool punk in Stephen King's *Christine.* He was obviously trying to sneak back out again.

"Hold it *right* there, dork man!"

Gordie froze, looked from side to side, then back at Libby as he pointed to his scrawny chest. "Me?"

"Do you see any other dorks in the room?" Libby asked sarcastically. "In fact, do you see anyone but us?"

Shaking his head, Gordie winced.

"And why is that?" Crossing her arms and narrowing her gaze, Libby pressed the interrogation. Like the countess from *Once Bitten* whom she had chosen to portray, there was a cunning, predatory quality to her slow advance that was guaranteed to intimidate. The short, shimmering black dress with long sleeves that flared at the cuff, black stockings, and high heels enhanced the image of power she always cultivated so carefully. The fake vampire fangs would have been a nice touch under the circumstances, but they were uncomfortable and she had slipped them into her evening bag after the first few guests had arrived.

"Everyone split for Sabrina's house, didn't they?"

Shrugging, Gordie started to sweat. "H-how would I-I know?"

"You're a nerd! You're smart. You know everything!" Although she didn't show it, Libby was pleased to note that Gordie, Jill, and Cee Cee cringed appropriately as her voice rose in mounting agitation. "So spit it out!"

"Yes!"

"Why?"

Wringing his hands, Gordie mumbled, "Because some-b-b-body called a-and said it was really—great."

"Great?" Libby snapped her entire body around to confront the two girls. "How could a party at Sabrina Spellman's possibly be great?"

Cee Cee and Jill both just shrugged.

Gordie bolted for the door and fled.

"Well—" Pausing to take a deep, calming breath, Libby sneered. "I guess we'll just have to drop by and find out, won't we?"

Jill gasped. "Surrender?"

"No," Libby said as a slow, malicious smile crept onto her face. "Sabotage."

☆

Chapter 12

☆

"Don't look so surprised, Sabrina."

Mortified, Sabrina clamped her jaw closed, which *had* dropped open when she answered the door and saw Libby, Cee Cee, and Jill standing on the porch. Vampire, teen witch, and Buffy the Vampire Slayer, the three girls dared her to turn them away with smug expressions and postures intended to intimidate.

There's never a huge, threatening butler around when you really need one, Sabrina mused.

Surprise, however, did not even begin to describe what she felt. Outraged indignation at Libby's audacious appearance after the cheerleader had tried and failed to destroy her party by secretly detouring the invited guests came close. Even so, Sabrina realized she would rather spend the rest of the evening picking lint off the mummy's moldy wrappings—if she could find him—than let Libby know she cared.

"You *did* invite us." Smiling with sinister sweetness, Libby and friends boldly stepped into the foyer.

"Come on in," Sabrina said graciously after the fact. Several caustic comments came to mind, but voicing them would be rising to Libby's bait. Ultimately, she'd get more mileage from a detached demeanor of unconcern.

Indifference was a powerful force.

And Libby applied it with particular aplomb.

"An interesting motif." Taking in the impressive monster-movie-set surroundings with an unflinching glance, Libby heaved an unimpressed sigh. "A bit overdone, but ancient musty castle does suit you. Just like that costume. Although Morticia's weirdness has a spark of sophistication that seems to be lacking."

"Thank you," Sabrina said simply, seething inside. "Black widow is highly appropriate for you, too."

Libby bristled ever so slightly.

"She's a vampire," Cee Cee said indignantly.

"Vampire. Spider. What's the difference? They both kill their mates." Sabrina shrugged and made an effort not to smile as Libby finally noticed that the house was overflowing with kids having a great time. A slight frown was the only indication that her poise had slipped a notch.

"Excuse us, Sabrina. We have better things to

do than making small talk in the hall." Taking her plastic fangs out of her purse, Libby changed her mind and dropped them back in. Then removing her short cape and slinging it over her shoulder, she prepared to make her grand entrance into the living room.

But Stagger made his first. Walking sedately out of the den, he loomed behind the three girls.

"The butler will take your cape and bag, Libby."

"Come off it, Sabrina. You don't have—" The cheerleader's cool evaporated with a gasp as she turned to find herself staring at Stagger's massive chest, and slowly shifted her gaze upward. "—a butler."

Cee Cee and Jill jumped back to cower against the wall.

Grunting, Stagger reached for Libby's things and growled when she yanked them away from his grasp.

"A word of advice, Libby," Sabrina whispered. "Let the butler do his job."

Shoving the cape and bag into Stagger's outstretched hands, Libby watched with indignant annoyance as he casually dropped them on the bottom step of the staircase, then calmly returned to his position by the door. Straightening again, she spun back around just as Hilda passed through on litter patrol.

Carrying a pile of used paper plates, Hilda stopped and did a double take. "Libby! What are you doing here?" Her head snapped toward Sabrina. "What's she doing here?"

"Oh, she just stopped in to eat, drink, and be merry," Sabrina quipped with a bright smile and a pointed look. "Like *everyone* else."

Hilda blinked, then grinned as the message sank in. She turned back to Libby. "Great party, isn't it?"

"I haven't been here long enough to know." Libby's scowl darkened as Brad Shaefer, star quarterback and absentee guest of honor at her defunct party, grabbed a complimentary monster mask off the hall table.

"Need some help?" Taking the paper plates from Hilda, Brad beamed at Sabrina. "This is a great party! In fact, this may be the best bash I've ever been to. Thanks."

"You're welcome."

Fuming as Brad followed Hilda to complete the trash rounds, Libby stalked into the living room. Spurred by Stagger's annoyed snarl, Jill and Cee Cee wasted no time following her.

Basking in the glory of her moral victory, Sabrina just laughed when Kevin O'Shea, wearing the grossly realistic face of the Cryptkeeper, walked by engaged in heavy conversation with the Frankenstein monster, who merely nodded and grunted to hold up his end and carried yet another plate heaped with food. Still following the trail of fumbled and dropped delicacies, Salem veered off when he spotted Sabrina and leaped into her arms.

"*This* is a great party." The cat burped.

"So I've heard." Scratching the gluttonous feline behind the ears, Sabrina asked, "Have you seen Harvey?"

"Not since he rescued some guy named Larry from being bored to death by Tomato Woman." Salem purred. "It seems she never got over her crush on Napoleon."

"Thanks for the warning."

"Don't mention it. Gotta go." Jumping down, Salem sped off after his monster meal ticket.

Now that everything was running smoothly and she no longer had to run interference between her mortal guests and the monsters, Sabrina realized she could relax and start to enjoy herself. It was only ten-thirty with plenty of party left to go. Besides, not only had Libby been put in her place by the party's unquestionable success, Aunt Vesta and her friends were controlling their mischievous impulses, too. In fact, things were going so well, it was scary.

She decided not to tempt fate by thinking about it, and went looking for Harvey.

The quiet and not-too-bright guy with the bolts sticking out of his neck should have been easy to find.

Wrong, Salem thought when the tidbit trail

ended where the giant klutz had dropped his empty plate in the den. *But not necessarily a major problem.*

Ever since the big fella had deposited the mummy on the dryer in the laundry room, he had made one circuit of the downstairs rooms after another without failing to stop for more food. On a good day, the trudging hulk couldn't reach the oasis of Orlando's exquisite culinary talents in the dining room ahead of a cat motivated by an insatiable hunger—even with a five-minute head start. Since it had only been two, Salem sat down to tidy up his luxurious coat.

"Wait! Where are you going?"

Salem started as Jenny the gypsy whirled to face the man who was desperately in need of good grooming. His unkempt hair, bushy sideburns, and beard were all growing longer at a phenomenal rate.

"Listen, Larry or whatever your name is—" Eyes flashing with an angry fire, Jenny jabbed the pathetic werewolf-in-progress in the chest with her finger. "If you don't get off this silver bullet kick and find someone else to harass, I'm gonna make you sorry you were ever born!"

"I'm already sorry! That's the point—"

"Scram!"

Way to go, Jenny. Salem applauded the girl's grit by sharpening his claws in the carpet, a feline indulgence that normally got him chased with a broom. However, given the number of real and fake clawed creatures in the house, neither Hilda nor Zelda could blame him for any damage. Not for sure.

Curious and secure in the knowledge that Frankenstein's monster would maintain his established routine, Salem padded after Larry when Jenny stormed back toward the living room.

"This is not in the script," the poor man muttered, dropping into a chair beside Vesta and the trick-or-treating zombie named Mark who were watching TV.

Correction. Super Secret Inside-a-Vision.

Salem crept up to sneak a peek at the TV set Vesta had turned into a device capable of being fine-tuned to spy on anyone she desired. No matter who Vesta and the boy were watching, the subject had to be more entertaining than the depressing wild-dog guy.

"She's making a fool of herself." Mark shook with quiet rage. "That creep doesn't want to have anything to do with Lynne."

Salem yawned. Watching the arrogant, pushy girl get the brush-off from the handsome young warlock in vampire's clothing was rewarding, especially since she had dragged Mark to Libby's, but it wasn't worth missing out on more food.

"True," Vesta agreed sympathetically. "Rafe prefers to do the chasing and he's a sucker for a girl who plays hard to get. Like that one."

Salem's eyes widened as Libby entered the field of view. The despicable girl tripped a scrawny kid with glasses. His plate tipped and the sandwich he had just made slid off onto the floor. "Turn up the volume!"

"Who said that?" Mark looked back and scowled at Larry, whose hairy face was buried in his hands.

"Who cares? This might be interesting." Vesta turned up the sound.

"—blame me, Gordie!" Libby stomped on without even looking at Rafe, which won her the warlock's instant and undivided attention. Sprinting to catch up, he jumped in front of her and bowed.

"Allow me to introduce myself—"

"Out of my way, jerk!" Libby snapped.

Furious, Lynne inserted herself between them. "Stay away from her, Rafe. She'd rather laugh in your face than tell you the time. She'll reject you, insult you, and make you feel like—"

"Shut up, Lynne," Libby barked.

Pretending to pull down his elegant cuff, Rafe snapped his wrist. "That's quite enough, Lynne. Thank you."

Lynne's hands flew to her throat. Her lips kept moving, but no sound came out.

"What just happened there?" Mark demanded.

"Nothing we can't fix," Vesta said with a dangerous lilt in her velvet voice. "If you insist."

Rolling her eyes, Libby pushed Rafe aside and stormed through the dining room. Salem watched the image pan until she disappeared into the kitchen with Rafe in slow and calm pursuit, then gasped. Frankenstein's monster was not at the table filling a plate with egg rolls and chicken wings!

Hightailing it for the living room, Salem hoped that snack man was just running ahead of schedule. Leaping onto the piano, he scanned the crowd, but there was no sign of him. Sabrina was laughing with Harvey, Jenny, and another odd couple on the far side of the room. Glad that she was finally enjoying herself, he decided not to interrupt. He couldn't talk to her with so many mortals around anyway. However, Helena was sitting on the piano bench, pouring her heart out to the skeleton.

"Have you seen the tall guy with the bolts?"

"No." Helena sniffled and pushed her wilting tomato-stem hat further back on her head. "I'm not into tall. Napoleon was short, you know. I invented elevated boots just for him—"

"I'm outta here." Salem jumped, expecting to land on the floor. His controlled descent was brought up short when he hit something soft and squishy that instantly began to envelop him. Hissing, spitting, and clawing his way free, he heard the larger-than-he-had-last-seen-it blob make a rumbling noise that sounded uncomfortably like his own growling stomach. He split, quickly removing himself as a potential entree for the creature's next meal.

Backtracking into the dining room and ducking

under the table, Salem checked out the feet shuffling around the buffet while he nibbled the ham and cheese sandwich Gordie had dropped. No mud-covered size-fifteen boots were in evidence. But Zelda's voice was unmistakable.

"Excuse me. I just want to refill the pizza squares."

Striking out in the dining room, Salem dashed into the kitchen fully expecting to find his primary food source dipping into one of Zelda's simmering pots. He was surprised to discover that the kitchen was just as crowded as the rest of the lower level, and darted under a chair to keep from being trampled.

Hilda and the football kid dumped a load of trash in the compacter, then headed out to collect more.

The moment Hilda was gone, Aunt Vesta opened the secret pantry and began rooting through the powders and potions.

Looking like a thunderstorm waiting for her cue to begin, Libby paced back and forth while the infatuated Rafe watched from a safe distance of several feet.

Mark, the jilted zombie, glared at Rafe.

And judging by the heavy legs and clunky shoes under the table with him, Catherine had decided to sit out the entire evening on a kitchen chair.

But no big guy.

Figuring he had just misjudged the monster's route and timing, Salem started to creep out from under the chair when someone banged on the back door. When no one else made a move to answer, Catherine did.

"Good evening. I am Count Dracula—"

"Whad'ya want?" Catherine asked impatiently.

"I want in."

"Tough." Slamming the door in his face, Catherine stomped back to her chair.

Salem sat down to wait out the crowd. Eventually, the hungry giant would make his way back to the kitchen.

Aunt Vesta finished mixing a potion to cure Lynne's sudden case of acute laryngitis and carried it to Rafe. "If you don't add your reversal approval to this, you'll spend next Halloween baby-sitting Amanda for Cousin Marigold."

If Rafe had not already drained some of the blood from his face to enhance his vampire image, he would have paled. He pointed instead.

"So wise for one so young." Motioning for Mark to follow her out, Vesta explained, "I took the liberty of adding a pinch of hog hoof for humility and just a touch of sycamore spice to warm up her heart."

"Don't I wish," Mark sighed.

Yawning, Salem curled up to grab forty winks—

"What is all that stuff?" Libby asked.

—then sat up again on red alert.

Libby strolled over to the secret pantry which Vesta had neglected to close, with the adoring

Rafe at her side. Grimacing as she took a tentative whiff from an open bottle on the counter, she glared at her fanged admirer. "Do these things taste as bad as they smell?"

"Worse."

"Really?" Reaching for a large container sitting in the sink, Libby picked up a tin of purple powder. "I think it's time to spike the punch."

"You are delightfully malicious for a mortal," Rafe said.

Whiskers and tail twitching, Salem prepared to bolt for the door, when Frankenstein's monster wandered in from the laundry room carrying the mummy. The cat hesitated, torn between not letting the morsel monster out of his sight again and warning Sabrina that Libby was about to brew up a disaster of unknown but potentially catastrophic proportions and effects.

During those few seconds, the monster placed the mummy in a chair by Catherine, then trudged over to the door when the banging started again. He let Count Dracula in.

Salem bolted.

And was snagged by the monster's huge hand.

While being slowly crushed in the gentle giant's affectionate embrace, Salem was alarmingly aware of everything that happened next.

Rafe added something to Libby's container of magic mayhem, then handed it back to her. They both headed for the dining room.

"What are you staring at?" Catherine glowered at the count, who discreetly lowered his gaze.

Startled, the big guy gasped and stumbled backward.

Still wrapped like a cocoon, the mummy toppled sideways off his chair onto the floor.

A whimper that Salem strongly suspected belonged to the Creature from the Black Lagoon came from the broom closet.

Bursting in through the living-room door, hairy Larry sputtered in panic. "Where's the gypsy girl who loves me? The script says—"

"Can it!" Incensed and disgusted, Catherine jumped up. "Since when do self-respecting monsters act like such wimps? You're a disgrace to your genre. All of you. Now start acting like your directors intended and go scare the living daylights out of all those stupid kids!"

Uh-oh.

As Frankenstein's monster roared and raised him over his head, Salem wondered if cats really did land on their feet *all* the time.

☆

Chapter 13

☆

Sabrina's first hint that all was not as well as she had thought hit her smack in the stomach just after the wall clock bonged eleven. Sitting on the floor in a corner with Harvey, Jenny, Richard, and Sarah, she was caught totally off guard when Salem leaped into her lap, then clawed his way up to whisper in her ear.

"Guest bathroom. Now! We've got to talk!"

"Okay, but what—"

Tail fluffed and hackles raised, the cat was gone in a flash of black fur.

"Looks like Salem's had a little too much catnip." Harvey winked.

"Too many egg rolls is more like it," Sabrina said.

A loud roar followed by several shrill squeals and a resounding crash rose from the dining room.

"And it sounds like this party is gearing up to wild!" Richard laughed.

"Too wild, maybe." Frowning, Sabrina stood up and brushed herself off. Leaving the crash investigation to her aunts, who had diligently kept a low profile except for an occasional trash run and restocking Orlando's warmers, she decided to check on the cat. "Be right back."

As she turned to leave, Harvey grabbed the hem of her black dress and spoke in his silky Gomez voice. "Don't be too long, Tish. Torture is so much better shared."

"I just love it when you talk pain." Staying in character for her exit, Sabrina threw Harvey a snarl and slowly walked away. As she rounded the corner into the foyer, she quickened her pace. She couldn't imagine what had spooked Salem so badly, but she hoped it was nothing more urgent than running out of shrimp egg rolls.

Whatever it was, though, it would have to wait. When Sabrina entered the den, she saw Aunt Vesta urging Lynne to drink a pink concoction with a subtle glow.

"Just gulp this down—"

"No, don't!" Hitching up her tight skirt, Sabrina dashed to snatch the mysterious drink from Vesta's hand before the liquid passed Lynne's lips. She ignored another series of screams, trusting Zelda and Hilda to handle the unruly guests while she dealt with Vesta. "What is this?"

"It's just a cure for laryngitis," Mark said.

Vesta's eyes narrowed with ominous meaning. "I think she *caught* it from *Rafe.*"

Sabrina's eyes widened with the realization that Vesta was attempting to undo a silence spell. She handed thc drink back. "Oh. *That* kind of laryngitis. Sorry."

Taking a deep breath, Lynne drained the glass, turned red, then coughed and sputtered. "That's awful!"

"Here you go." Appearing on the fringe of the small group, Libby handed Lynne a plastic cup of Hocus-pocus Punch. "Maybe this will help wash it down."

"Thanks." Lynne gratefully gulped the green beverage.

Moving on with a sly smile planted on her face and an amused Rafe glued to her side, Libby cast Sabrina a sidelong glance. "Great party."

"What's that supposed to mean?" If Libby answered, Sabrina didn't hear. Her gaze was drawn back to Lynne when Mark and Vesta both gasped.

"That's much better." Smiling because her voice had returned, Lynne didn't realize her perfectly straight, pearly white teeth had suddenly become chipped and crooked and were turning black. "What's wrong?"

"Your teeth—" Mark shrank back in disgust.

Putting her hand to her mouth, Lynne inhaled with a stricken cry and bolted for the bathroom.

"What did you put in that, Aunt Vesta?" Sabrina demanded hotly.

"Nothing that would have *that* kind of effect!" Bewildered, Aunt Vesta shrugged. "Witch's honor."

"Really?" Sabrina hesitated for a split second, then dashed after Lynne. Aunt Vesta wouldn't lie on her witch's word, but somebody had obviously been fooling around with some pretty vile magic. Since the girl had been hounding Rafe, the warlock was the most likely suspect, but Sabrina wanted more information before she confronted him.

Just as Lynne reached the bathroom, the Creature from the Black Lagoon raced out of the dining room. Screeching and waving his scaly green arms, he leaped in front of the door. Faced off with the amphibious nightmare, Lynne matched his high-pitched screech, then keeled over in a dead faint.

The teens hanging out in the den stopped laughing.

Letting Mark handle his fallen girlfriend, Sabrina rushed the berserk creature. She didn't know what his problem was, but Hilda was to blame. Her aunt had sworn that the conjured movie monsters were harmless. Setting her finger to stun, Sabrina aimed.

Still screeching, the creature threw a protective arm over his ugly face, then opened the bathroom door and backed inside. Yowling, Salem barely made it out between the monster's webbed feet before the door slammed and locked from the inside.

"What's with that guy?" Pulling off a hard plastic alien mask, Brad exhaled in disgust.

In the upstairs bathroom directly above, the Romanian something howled and began throwing itself against the door.

"He's a method actor," Sabrina explained as she picked up the terrified cat huddled against her leg. Whimpering, Salem stuffed his head in the crook of her arm. "Guess he just got a little *too* into his part."

"If I were you, I'd dock his pay." Lifting a glass of punch off the loaded tray Stagger carried by, Brad took a healthy swallow. "In fact, I'd fire him on the—" The football player sneezed, then sneezed again and again.

Seizing the opportunity to escape without offending him, Sabrina turned toward the dining room to find her aunts. She wanted Zelda's assurance that the unhappy and unknown being upstairs was being contained by a ward spell and not solely by an ordinary bathroom door. And Aunt Hilda would have to send her strange assortment of film stars packing—she hoped before another one reverted to type.

Ducking into the dining room, Sabrina hugged the cat to steady herself and stared in paralyzed disbelief.

Too late.

Hunched with his teeth bared and fists raised, Frankenstein's monster stood in front of the table, defending the captured buffet. After two hours of forty teenagers helping themselves, Orlando's elegant array of platters and bowls had long since ceased to be elegant, but the once appetizing spread was nothing but monster-mushed garbage now. One of the warmers lay on the floor beside the huge hulk, which explained the crash Sabrina had heard earlier. Judging from the lack of food around the dented silver server, it had been empty.

Every kid in the room watched without moving or making a sound for fear the massive creature would fly into another raging tantrum.

Except Gordie. Looking warily back over his shoulder as he came in, and oblivious to the B-movie drama taking place, the science whiz and likable nerd reached for a paper plate. When the furious monster began pelting him with sandwich rolls, Gordie fled back the way he had come.

The rolls bounced off Stagger, who didn't even flinch as he walked in with the empty serving tray balanced on his shoulder and went to the caldron to load up with more Hocus-pocus Punch.

"Enough is enough." Devastated by the sudden ruin of what had been an almost perfect party, Sabrina's shock gave way to anger. Shifting the quivering Salem into one arm, she pointed to subdue the monster with a stun spell and gasped as Aunt Zelda grabbed her arm.

"Don't!" her aunt warned.

"Why not? He's wrecking everything!"

Ignoring her outraged protest, Zelda pulled Sabrina into the kitchen where Hilda was pacing and wringing her hands. Stone-faced Catherine was still sitting at the table—with Count Dracula.

"Who let him in?" Not really caring, Sabrina focused her fury on Hilda. "The monsters are going crazy! Get rid of them. Please!"

"I can't. Not until we figure out what went wrong."

Seeing Hilda's pained expression, Sabrina forced herself to calm down. Her aunt was honestly upset about the horrible turn the party had taken, and nothing would be accomplished by exploding and making her feel worse. Still, she was the only one who could solve the problem. "I don't understand. You brought them here."

"Yes, she did," Zelda said. "But she also modified their behavior so they wouldn't hurt anyone."

"Then why are they attacking my friends?"

"I don't know," Hilda whined. "That's the problem. Either I've lost my ability to control my magic or someone tampered with my spell."

"Until we know which," Zelda said soberly, "Hilda's grounded. Unstable and erratic magic is too dangerous to risk using."

"Having a bunch of movie monsters rampaging

around the house is not exactly safe," Sabrina pointed out.

Salem raised his head and hissed softly. "Catherine did it."

Sabrina, Hilda, and Zelda all started, then turned as the aging and obsolete Count Dracula rose from his chair. Spreading his cape and baring his gleaming fangs, he hissed with menace.

"You call that scary?" Catherine fixed the dated count with a bored stare and yawned.

Insulted and outraged, Dracula spun on his heels and stormed out of the kitchen as Hilda stormed up to the short, dumpy witch who had dared to meddle with her magic. She did not mince words.

"How did you override my spell and turn my harmless movie monsters into the fiends they really are, Catherine?"

"I didn't use a spell. I just gave them a pep talk so they'd stop acting like spineless ninnies and start wreaking havoc like they're supposed to. I was quite inspiring."

"Apparently," Sabrina snapped back, wincing as more screams sounded throughout the house.

"So my safeguard spell didn't work." Hilda paled and sank into the chair the count had vacated. "I'm ruined."

Jumping out of Sabrina's arms and into Hilda's lap, Salem purred. "There are worse fates than losing your powers. At least, you're not a cat, too."

Sabrina didn't know what to say so she didn't say anything. Given Aunt Hilda's problem, worrying about a party that had become the social debacle of the century seemed petty and selfish. Except for the fact that her friends were in dire danger.

"I don't think we should jump to any conclusions until we consult with a doctor." Zelda closed her eyes and raised her arms to place the call.

"You expect to reach a witch doctor on Halloween?" Catherine burst out laughing. "What a joke!"

Sabrina failed to see the humor in Hilda's situation or her own. Which seemed to be getting worse, she thought as Harvey charged in from the living room. With his ruffled hair, rumpled suit, and askew tie, he looked as if he had fought his way to the kitchen. And, she realized aghast, he probably had!

Shaken, Harvey stammered breathlessly, "You'd better get back out there, Sabrina. Something really strange is going on!"

Hilda looked up sharply. "Define strange."

"Well, aside from having to wrestle some guy who looks like a big shaggy dog to get in here, it's like there's a weird plague breaking out all of a sudden." Frightened and perplexed, Harvey took a deep breath. "Like everyone's allergies have flared up or something."

Zelda started for the door. "Like what exactly?"

Harvey shrugged. "Well, like Jill and Cee Cee started itching all over and Brad can't stop sneezing."

Startled, Salem rose on his hind legs to whisper in Hilda's ear. She stood up suddenly, dumping the cat off her lap. "The punch! Libby—" She cast a guarded glance at Harvey, then pointed at the open potion cabinet. *"—spiked* the punch!"

Zelda's mouth fell open. "But she couldn't have empowered the active ingredients!"

"No," Hilda said, "but Rafe could."

"Oh, no!" Grabbing Harvey's hand as she flew by, Sabrina darted back into the dining room. Passing her, Hilda and Zelda ran to the cauldron to prevent anyone else from drinking the badly bewitched brew.

Chaos didn't even begin to describe what was happening.

Frankenstein's monster continued to guard the table he had taken hostage, but, Sabrina realized to her horror, his aggressive defense was unnecessary. Although a few lucky kids who hadn't partaken of the altered punch huddled together in a corner for their mutual protection, several others were afflicted with a number of maladies that ranged from annoying to totally disgusting. Red rashes, hair loss, sneezing, and itching seemed to be the most prevalent manifestations, but there were isolated cases of extremely bizarre and gross effects, too. All of which were complicated by terror as the movie monsters ran amok.

With Harvey still in tow, Sabrina raced to check out the den. The situation there was just as bad, if not worse. Gordie cringed in a corner, trapped by the mummy who was still completely wrapped but managing to cut off the boy's escape by hopping up and down to block him. A hysterical girl who had grown a third eye in the middle of her forehead tried to run into the bathroom to hide, and rebounded off the locked door onto her butt. Watching with rapt interest, Aunt Vesta unlocked and opened the door with a quick point. The water creature in the small bathroom renewed his earsplitting screeching when he spotted the three-eyed girl.

"What's going on here?" Harvey asked as Sabrina skirted a boy who was hopelessly tangled in his own hair, which had grown to incredible lengths in a matter of seconds and continued to grow.

"That's what I'd like to know!" Although she had no hope of returning to a normal life in the wake of the disastrous party, Sabrina still had to set things right before she was run out of town. And that meant going to the source of the problem. "Where's Rafe, Aunt Vesta?"

"Is all this delightful madness his doing?" Vesta beamed proudly, then quickly frowned when she realized Sabrina was not pleased. "The last time I saw him he was headed for the living room."

A girl trying to escape the aged Count Dracula, who seemed driven to prove he could still frighten someone, ran up in a panic. "Help me!"

"Certainly." Smiling, Vesta snapped her wrist and a string of garlic appeared around the girl's neck. Shrieking even louder, the girl ran on.

Sabrina pointed at the pursuing vampire. Tripping over his own feet, Dracula fell flat on his face and pounded the floor with his fists in a fit of frustration.

"This is not happening," Harvey muttered.

Since Sabrina couldn't possibly explain, it seemed senseless to try. She just pulled him into the foyer where the almost totally converted Wolfman was beating on the coat closet door, simultaneously pleading and roaring with rage.

"But you're *supposed* to save me! Come out!"

"I don't care! Go away!"

Although the heavy door muffled Jenny's voice, Sabrina recognized it immediately. At her wits' end and desperate, she yelled, "Yo! Larry!" As the furious werewolf whirled around to face her, she spat out a sharp command: "Sit!"

He sat.

"Stay!" Leaving Jenny safely locked inside the closet and the obedient werewolf sitting on the floor, Sabrina ran into the living room and skidded to a horrified halt.

Ned Wallace, editor and basketball player, was frantically trying to chase off a throng of bats swooping down on him from the walls.

Sitting on top of the piano and weeping into her microphone, Helena crooned an old melancholy pop tune called "When Sunny Gets Blue" in a soprano voice that cracked repeatedly. The skeleton in top hat and tails had been animated and swayed in time to the accompaniment he played with his long bony fingers. A dozen kids afflicted with everything from purple blotches to painful hangnails were gathered around her, a captive audience held in place by yet another forbidden spell.

Wandering in from the kitchen still clutching her handbag, Catherine peered into the apple-dunking barrel. With a casual point she sent a bolt of electricity into the water which convinced the even-bigger, bulging blob to come tumbling out. She giggled as the pulsing mass slithered into the kitchen with an amazing alacrity.

"Catherine's laughing!" Vesta exclaimed as she glided up beside Sabrina.

"Yeah," Harvey said, keeping his cool despite the inexplicable and fantastic happenings around him. "But she's got a really dark sense of humor."

"No matter." Vesta grinned. "Her shrink didn't specify what kind of sense of humor the miserable little party pooper had to awaken. I'm off the hook."

Spotting Rafe and Libby in the far corner, Sabrina leveled Vesta with a no-nonsense stare. "Watch Harvey and do *not* let anything weird happen to him."

"Nothing weird?" Harvey blinked at Vesta as Sabrina stalked off. "What does she call all this?"

Vesta shrugged. "I don't know, but I call it a great Halloween party."

Squaring her shoulders and braced for a showdown, Sabrina pushed through the crowd of catatonic or crying victims of Rafe's perverse Halloween prank. When she reached him and his mortal accomplice, Libby couldn't wait to gloat.

"Well, Sabrina. As everyone was saying earlier, this is one party no one will forget for a long, long time. Just not for the reasons you hoped."

Refusing to give Libby the satisfaction of knowing how right she was and how much it hurt, Sabrina targeted Rafe. "Are the effects of that punch you poisoned permanent or will they wear off?"

Rafe shrugged. "I haven't decided yet."

"Poisoned?" Libby's smug smile faded. "Permanent? You didn't tell me the effects of that allergy stimulator we made might be permanent!"

"Please be quiet, Libby." Rafe sighed. "You're giving me a headache."

"Stuff it, you overly polite, arrogant—"

Rolling his eyes, Rafe pointed. Libby's canine

teeth instantly elongated into vampire fangs that prevented her from talking without puncturing her own tongue and lip.

"—twerp! Ouch!" Gasping, Libby pressed back against the wall and froze in wide-eyed fright.

"Decide, Rafe!" Sabrina hissed through gritted teeth. "And don't even *think* the word *permanent!*"

"It doesn't really matter one way or the other."

The whole house shook as Drell's booming voice echoed through it and the head of the Witches' Council made his dramatic entrance. With a flash of lightning and a crash of thunder, he appeared in the center of the room garbed in flowing, shimmering robes.

Sabrina and Rafe flinched.

The mortal teenagers ducked, then stared.

Abandoning their watch over the cauldron, Hilda and Zelda came running. The Frankenstein monster lumbered in behind them, gnawing on an oversize turkey leg they must have zapped up to pacify him. The blob oozed into the kitchen doorway and flattened.

"But it does matter!" Sabrina insisted, breaking the pervasive stunned silence that gripped everyone.

"No. It doesn't." Wagging an annoyed finger, Drell froze the moment, the scene, the monsters, and the mortal contingent. Salem ran for the dining room while the witches held their collective breath.

"Why not?" Sabrina asked hopefully. Maybe the powerful warlock had magnanimously decided to reverse time so she could do the party over from its promising beginning.

"Because none of these mortals are leaving this house."

"Oh." Checking a sudden panic, Sabrina risked asking one more question. "For how long?"

Drell smiled. "Forever."

☆

Chapter 14

☆

"You can't be serious." Sabrina laughed shortly, then coughed to cover the blunder when Drell frowned.

"Generally speaking, I avoid being serious whenever possible." Shaking out his long dark hair and adjusting his robe, Drell scowled. "This is *not* one of those times."

Moving up to flank her on the right, Hilda patted Sabrina's shoulder. Her aunt's tight-lipped smile was not reassuring.

"Don't panic just yet," Zelda whispered in her left ear. "I'm sure someday we'll look back on this and laugh."

Yeah, right, Sabrina thought grimly. *From exile in the Other Realm.*

Rafe, Helena, and Catherine nervously gathered behind Aunt Vesta, perfectly willing to let the glamorous and daring free spirit take the brunt of Drell's wrath should it descend upon them.

"But what's the problem?" Sabrina asked.

"The problem?" Laughing, the warlock began to wander through the mass of teenagers time-frozen in various poses and phases of fright in the Spellman living room. "This one has an interesting rash." Drell traced the outline of a huge blotch on a zombie girl's bare upper back. "It's shaped like Ireland. And that one—" He indicated a boy dressed in a black leather jacket and jeans with a silver robot mask stuffed in his pocket. "—seems to have lost all his hair. Unless he was always bald." Drell looked at Sabrina for confirmation.

"No, he wasn't, actually."

"I didn't think so." Moving on, Drell paused to study the contorted faces of Jill the Vampire Slayer and Cee Cee the hot teen witch, whose arms and bodies were bent at odd angles. "These two seem to be engaged in scratching a mysterious and serious itch." His gaze shifted to the boy standing next to them. "And here we have a young man looking at his teeth, which have recently fallen out of his mouth and into his hand."

"I know all that," Sabrina said impatiently. "But what's the problem? Besides the obvious one."

Snapping his head around, Drell bellowed. "The problem is that most of your mortal friends here are suffering from some sudden and horrible affliction that cannot be explained within the limits of the mortal world's normal operating parameters!"

"So?" Confused, Sabrina was just looking for clarification. However, her impudent tone triggered a greater degree of anger.

"So?" Drell's face flushed and his eyes flashed as he blasted Sabrina with a question of his own. "So what are they going to think happened here, huh?"

Shaken and certain that whatever she said would be wrong, Sabrina shrugged.

Drell was not placated. "Magic! That's how they'll explain it. Magic!"

Rafe cringed as Drell impaled him with a knowing glance. Catherine and Helena averted their guilty gazes and Aunt Vesta smiled. Zelda just sighed.

"Calm down, Drell," Hilda admonished. "Getting angry and upset won't solve anything."

Fuming but regaining his cool, Drell graced his old flame with a tolerant smile. "It's Halloween, Hilda. I'd rather be somewhere else having fun. I *was* somewhere else having fun. And now I'm not. I'm here trying to fix this mess because it's my job as head of the Witches' Council. I'll get as upset and angry as I please. Understood?"

"Of course," Hilda flared. "I never could reason with you. Why should now be any different?"

"You've still got fire, Hilda." A thoughtful

frown replaced Drell's admiring smile. "Why did we break up again?"

Desperate and wanting to get back to the real reason for Drell's unannounced visit before her Aunt Hilda said or did something she'd regret, Sabrina ventured a suggestion. "So why not just *solve* the problem with magic so everyone can go home and get on with their lives?"

"Like what, for instance?" Crossing his arms, Drell paced back and forth in front of her. "Come on. Let's have it. I'm listening."

"Time reversal would be a quick and easy fix."

"Sorry. That's an extreme measure reserved to help witches out of cruel and unusual circumstances with lifelong repercussions—not mortals."

"But I—"

"Forget it, Sabrina," Drell said. "I've already stretched the rules once to help you salvage your mortal social life. Besides, after I've changed everyone here into some kind of animal, there won't be anyone around to talk about your botched party, and your precious reputation won't be harmed. Next idea."

Fresh out of ideas, Sabrina tried a counterargument. "But witches go out and use magic to harass mortals all the time. Especially on Halloween."

"Quite true. But we confine our activities to small groups or individuals and we exercise discretion. There are forty witnesses to the effects of the magic used in this house tonight, and Rafe let that Libby person help him brew the potion!"

So much for the everyone-else-does-it defense. It didn't work on warlocks any better than it did on parents or guardian aunts.

Sabrina resorted to begging. "But why do you have to turn them into anything? Why can't we just undo the spells and let them talk? No one will believe them!"

"Now that's where you're wrong." Drell's voice rose to emphasize the point.

"Drell," Zelda said patiently. "You're not worried that these kids are going to spark another round of witch hunts and burnings, are you?"

"Burnings? No. Hunts? Yes." Drell sighed. "But a modern witch-hunt would be far worse than anything witches suffered in colonial America."

"Worse than being chased down, tried and convicted on flimsy evidence, and burned at the stake?" Hilda blinked. "How do you figure that?"

Dropping onto the couch beside Brad Shaefer, who had become immobile halfway through a sneeze, Drell lapsed into lecture mode. "Back then, mortals were afraid of witches. Now they *want* to believe. There's forty kids here, Hilda. If they talk about what happened tonight—which they will—someone will believe them. And life for us will never be the same."

"I *still* don't see the problem." Sabrina huffed in frustration.

"Then let me explain it." Drell made glowing blue slashes in the air to tally his examples. "Demeaning, fabricated articles in the tabloids. Being hounded by talk show hosts to appear on their programs, and then, if anyone is stupid enough to agree, being subjected to humiliating questioning and debunking on the air. But worst of all, being pursued by fanatics just like those devoted to UFOs, who are determined to prove our existence."

"He does paint a pretty ugly picture," Vesta said.

"Unfortunately," Zelda agreed.

With forty teenaged lives at stake, Sabrina could not give up the fight. Remembering how Drell had agreed to let Jenny resume her life as a girl after he turned her into a grasshopper, she knew he might be swayed if she came up with a viable plan. She and her aunts had saved Jenny by making her believe her very real Other Realm experience was all a dream. That wouldn't work this time, but she had another idea that just might do the trick.

"Can I ask another question?"

Drell rolled his eyes. "Nothing's stopped you so far."

"If I can explain everything that's happened so it fits the mortal world's operating rules and my friends buy it, will you let them go?"

"Sure. You can't, of course, but watching you

try might be amusing." Drell raised his hand to start the clock again.

"Wait." Sabrina stopped him. "All the spells have to be removed the instant time begins moving forward again."

Drell passed the buck. "That decision belongs to the witches who cast them."

"I just used an electric prod on a slimy thing," Catherine said.

Helena shrugged, then nodded when Vesta nudged her in the ribs. "I really didn't care for that skeleton's piano style, anyway."

"Rafe's spiked punch was responsible for most of the damage," Zelda mused. "And that might present a problem because it was ingested—not pointed."

"Actually," Rafe said pleasantly, "it's no problem at all. I used a worst-nightmare powder for the base and mass-hysteria sugar as the catalyst. I can neutralize the effects by simply snapping my fingers."

"Will you?" Sabrina asked.

"Absolutely. As a personal favor to you, Sabrina. It was a great party and I had a wonderful time."

"Thanks." It would be nice if her other guests felt the same way when all was said and done, but getting everyone out of the house alive and human was more important.

"What about you, Vesta?" Zelda's face darkened with warning.

"What's one less garlic necklace?" Vesta winked at Sabrina. "No problem here, either."

"But I have a problem." Hilda lowered her eyes. "The seal on my monster control spell didn't hold and I'm not sure I *can* point them out of existence."

"Hilda!" Drell gasped.

"Actually," Sabrina said quickly, "I don't think that's a problem. For one thing, the monsters have to stick around awhile."

"And for another?" Hilda asked hopefully.

"Your seal *did* hold." When Hilda opened her mouth to argue, Sabrina rushed into her explanation. "Even though they went a little crazy after Catherine's pep talk, your monsters didn't hurt anyone."

"But they tried."

"Not really, Aunt Hilda. The Creature from the Black Lagoon is hiding in the bathroom. The wolfman just wanted Jenny to follow the script, the mummy can barely move, and old Count Dracula needed to know that he hadn't lost his touch. And neither the blob nor Frankenstein's monster ate anything that wasn't already dead."

"Good point." Hilda glowed with relief. "No pun intended."

"Can we get on with it?" Drell urged.

"I really wish you would," Salem said. The thoroughly disgusted cat sat on the flattened blob in the kitchen doorway. "Time-frozen food cannot be moved or eaten."

Sabrina nodded. "As soon as I explain my plan and Aunt Hilda has a brief conference with her monsters."

Here goes nothing.

Sabrina took a deep breath as she and Rafe positioned themselves back in the corner with Libby. Everyone else returned to where they had been when Drell put time on hold. To her surprise, the blustering, powerful warlock had actually seemed eager to cooperate. But then, he had a starring role.

Fluffing his hair and smoothing his robes, Drell raised his hand, scanned the expectant witch faces awaiting their cue, then waved his hand.

Rafe snapped his fingers within the next split second, instantly removing all traces of the spiked punch's aftereffects from his victims.

Since almost everyone had been staring in awed fear at the tall man in long robes who had flashed into their midst when time stopped, it took a moment for Sabrina to realize that time had been reactivated.

"What happened to my teeth?" Still plastered against the wall, horrified by the fangs she had sprouted, Libby looked frantically between Sabrina and Rafe. The cheerleader had not yet realized that her teeth were fine.

"You left them in your purse," Sabrina said.

Maintaining a magnificently dignified pose,

Drell hesitated before launching into his impromptu speech, giving his bewildered and frightened audience a moment to discover that the terrible afflictions had vanished as quickly and mysteriously as they had appeared. The sighs and nervous giggles that swept the downstairs rooms were silenced when Drell shoved his fists into the air.

Herded out of the other rooms by Vesta and Zelda, the rest of the dazed and puzzled guests wandered in and found places to stand or sit and watch.

"Beware the powers of the mind! Your own—so easily manipulated. While mine commands the forces of wondrous deception." Drell's voice dropped to a sinister whisper and a tense hush fell over the crowd. "Beware your eyes, for they can deceive. What is real? What is not? Can you tell?"

Intrigued, relieved, and mesmerized, the crowd began to relax. One by one, Hilda's monsters slipped away unnoticed.

"What is reality?" Drell went on. "It is not set in stone, but shifts like windblown sands, ever-changing and unique to each individual's experience and perception."

"All right, already," Sabrina muttered, wishing the warlock would wind things up.

"Who is that weird guy?" Libby sneered.

"A friend," Rafe said. "Do shut up, won't you?"

"The hypnotic hallucination can seem so real."

Drell paused for dramatic effect. "Perhaps it was."

"Hypnotic?" Libby frowned.

A voice rose from the audience. "Are you saying that we were all hypnotized into believing a bunch of really strange stuff was happening?"

"You mean I didn't go bald?" The robot boy reached up, then grinned as he felt the hair on his head.

Drell just smiled, bowed, then straightened. "And that concludes this performance by Horror Party, Incorporated. Thank you for being such good sports!"

Sabrina tensed during the long, quiet moment that followed, waiting for her teen guests to save themselves or seal their own doom. Then suddenly, the silence was shattered by a cacophony of cheers, whistles, and applause.

Applauding with them, Drell waved the monsters to enter from the kitchen where they had just assembled as instructed. "Let's hear it for the monsters!"

Moving in single file, the six movie monsters eased through the crowd to stand by Drell. Waving and bowing—if their anatomy allowed—they basked in the enthusiastic appreciation of the wildly cheering teens.

"How do you think the blob works?" a young werewolf asked Gordie. "Remote control?"

"To be honest, I don't really want to know." Gordie hooted and clapped harder.

Sabrina finally relaxed when Drell gave her a thumbs-up as he and the monsters headed back toward the kitchen. *Home free.* With her friends' lives and her reputation saved, she did not even flinch when Libby exploded behind her.

"You had some creep hypnotize us? And hired actors to scare us all to death? Of all the sneaky, cheap—"

Libby's opinion and heated words were lost in the ensuing barrage of shouted compliments and congratulations that assailed her and the sounds of a great party gearing back up to not quite so wild.

"So," Hilda asked as Sabrina finally broke free of her friends and dashed into the kitchen ten minutes later. "How's it going out there? Are the monsters still behaving themselves?"

"Fabulous! And yes, they're having a great time being liked." Dropping into a chair at the table, Sabrina heaved a huge sigh. "If it's okay with you, let's give everyone about fifteen minutes to chill. Then you can come out and judge the costumes."

"Okay by me." Hilda smiled. "Have you seen Salem?"

Sabrina nodded. "He's chasing bats in the living room."

"You look tired." Pouring herself a cup of coffee, Zelda sat down beside her.

"I am a little," Sabrina admitted. "But everyone is so impressed. This couldn't have gone better if we had planned it. Except several people have already asked me for Horror Party, Incorporated's phone number."

"Really?" Leaning on the counter munching meatballs off a crystal plate, Drell looked up with interest. "Now that's a business opportunity that bears some serious consideration."

"After we finish celebrating Halloween, Drell." Aunt Vesta entered from the dining room with Catherine, Helena, and Rafe.

"It's almost midnight, Vesta. The holiday's over."

"Not on the West Coast!" With a bright smile and looking as fresh as she had when she arrived, Vesta threw Sabrina a kiss. Then taking Drell's arm, she and the other uninvited witches popped out to enjoy three more hours of Halloween havoc in California.

"It was really nice of Drell to help us out like that," Sabrina said. Convincing everyone they had been hypnotized as part of the Horror Party thrills and chills package might not have been so easy without Drell's stellar performance. And true to his word, he had reversed his initial decision to change them all into creepy-crawly things.

"Don't remind me." Hilda frowned. "After loving and leaving him centuries ago, I've learned to really *like* despising him. If you don't mind, I prefer to believe he has some diabolical ulterior motive that we're just not aware of yet."

"Well, if you don't mind, I think I'll get back to my friends." Sabrina's smile widened as she stood up and saw Harvey standing shyly in the doorway. Behind him, Jenny was shaking her tambourine and dancing with the Wolfman, whose happy howl was answered by a plaintive call from the upstairs bathroom.

"I'm sure it'll go back to Romania when I return the stones." Zelda frowned uncertainly. "I hope."

Sabrina's attention was on Harvey as he smoothed back his hair and walked toward her with Gomez's intensity. Putting on her calm and cold Morticia face, she eagerly settled into character to await his next move.

"Excuse me," Harvey said with an apologetic look at Sabrina's aunts when he stopped before her. "But I've *got* to do this."

Totally unprepared, Sabrina's breath caught in her throat as he swept her into his arms, dipped her backward, and treated her to a long and sensuous kiss.

"Harvey!" Sabrina gasped with astounded delight.

"Happy Halloween, Sabrina."

About the Author

Diana G. Gallagher lives in Minnesota with her husband, Marty Burke, three dogs, three cats, and a cranky parrot. When she's not writing, she likes to read, walk the dogs, and look for cool stuff at garage sales for her grandsons, Jonathan, Alan, and Joseph.

Diana and Marty are musicians who perform traditional and original Irish and American folk music at coffeehouses and conventions around the country. Marty sings and plays the twelve-string guitar and banjo. In addition to singing backup harmonies, Diana plays rhythm guitar and a round, Celtic drum called a *bodhran.*

A Hugo Award–winning artist, Diana is best known for her series *Woof: The House Dragon.* Her first adult novel, *The Alien Dark,* appeared in 1990. She and Marty coauthored *The Chance Factor,* a STARFLEET ACADEMY VOYAGER book. In addition to other STAR TREK novels for intermediate readers, Diana has written many books in other series published by Minstrel Books, including *The Secret World of Alex Mack, Are You Afraid of the Dark,* and *The Mystery Files of Shelby Woo.* She is currently working on original young adult novels for the Archway Paperback series, *Sabrina, the Teenage Witch.*

Sabrina, The Teenage Witch™ Sweepstakes Official Rules:

1. No Purchase Necessary. Enter by mailing the completed Official Entry Form or by mailing on a 3" x 5" card your name, address and daytime telephone number to Pocket Books/Sabrina, The Teenage Witch Sweepstakes, 13th Floor, 1230 Avenue of the Americas, NY, NY 10020. Entries must be received by 7/1/98. Not responsible for lost, late, damaged, stolen, illegible, mutilated, incomplete, not delivered entries or for typographical errors in the entry form or rules. Entries are void if they are in whole or in part illegible, incomplete or damaged. Enter as often as you wish, but each entry must be mailed separately. Winners will be selected at random from all eligible entries received in a drawing to be held on or about 7/7/98. Winners will be notified by mail.
2. Prizes: One Grand Prize: A weekend (four days/three nights) trip to Los Angeles for two people (the winning minor and one parent or legal guardian) including round-trip coach airfare from the major airport nearest the winner's residence, ground transportation or car rental, meals, three nights in a hotel (one room, occupancy for two) and a tour of the set of "Sabrina, The Teenage Witch" (approximate retail value $3500.00) and a savings bond worth $1000 ($US) upon maturity in 18 years. Travel accommodations are subject to availability; certain restrictions apply. 10 First Prizes: Sabrina's Cauldron filled with one CD-ROM (a Windows 95 compatible program), one set of eight Sabrina, The Teenage Witch books published by Archway Paperbacks, one set of three Simon & Schuster Children's books and one Hasbro Sabrina fashion doll (approximate retail value $100). 25 Second Prizes: Sabrina, The Teenage Witch CD-ROM published by Simon & Schuster Interactive (approximate retail value $30). 50 Third Prizes: Sabrina doll (approximate retail value $17.99). 100 Fourth Prizes: a one-year subscription of Sabrina, The Teenage Witch comic books published by Archie Comics (approximate retail value $15). The Grand Prize must be taken on the dates specified by sponsors.
3. The sweepstakes is open to legal residents of the U.S. and Canada (excluding Quebec). Prizes will be awarded to the winner's parent or legal guardian if under 18. Any minor taking a Grand Prize trip must be accompanied by a parent or legal guardian. Void in Puerto Rico and wherever prohibited or restricted by law. All federal, state and local laws apply. Employees of Viacom International, Inc., their families living in the same household, and its subsidiaries and their affiliates and their respective agencies and participating retailers are not eligible.
4. One prize per person or household. Prizes are not transferable and may not be substituted except by sponsors, in event of unavailability, in which case a prize of equal or greater value will be awarded. All prizes will be awarded. The odds of winning a prize depend upon the number of eligible entries received.
5. If a winner is a Canadian resident, then he/she must correctly answer a skill-based question administered by mail.
6. All expenses on receipt and use of prize including federal, state and local taxes are the sole responsibility of the winners. Winners may be required to execute and return an Affidavit of Eligibility and Release and all other legal documents which the sweepstakes sponsor may require (including a W-9 tax form) within 15 days of attempted notification or an alternate winner will be selected. Winner's travel companions will be required to execute a liability release prior to ticketing.
7. By accepting a prize, winners or winners' parents on winners' behalf agree to allow use of their names, photographs, likenesses, and entries for any advertising, promotion and publicity purposes without further compensation to or permission from the entrants, except where prohibited by law.
8. By participating in this sweepstakes, entrants agree to be bound by these rules and the decisions of the judges and sweepstakes sponsors, which are final in all matters relating to the sweepstakes.
9. The sweepstakes sponsors shall have no liability for any injury, loss or damage of any kind arising out of participation in this sweepstakes or the acceptance or use of the prize.
10. For a list of major prize winners, (available after 7/15/98) send a stamped, self-addressed envelope to Prize Winners, Pocket Books/Sabrina, The Teenage Witch Sweepstakes, 13th Floor, 1230 Avenue of the Americas, NY, NY 10020.